ONE
-ON- *A NOVEL*
ONE

ONE
-ON-
ONE

A NOVEL

# MICHAEL KELSO

WordCrafts

**One-on-One** is a work of fiction. All references to persons, places or events are fictitious or used fictitiously.

Published by WordCrafts Press
Buffalo, Wyoming 82834
www.wordcrafts.net

*Revenge is an act of passion, vengeance of justice.*
*Injuries are revenged; crimes are avenged.*
—Samuel Johnson


*My father once told me that character is judged by*
*how you treat those you don't have to treat well.*

*I never understood that saying.*
—Emil Sorn

# Preface

Corrections officers have a difficult job. They are called upon to enforce rules on those who have little or no regard for rules. They are vilified by those in their care as well as those who don't understand what's involved in the job they do.

When I was a C.O. there were certain things that you could only talk to another C.O. about. Friends, family, even spouses can't understand if they've never worked in corrections. The job they do is one of the most dangerous of any profession. It can have long lasting psychological and physiological repercussions. The stress they endure every day is among the highest of any career, and yet 98% of them do it day in and day out with the highest level of professionalism. They not only watch the inmates, they teach, mentor, coach, counsel, and discipline them. They receive as much if not more training than other law enforcement agencies, for less pay and less appreciation.

98% of the good things that C.O.s do is forgotten when the 2% that do something wrong are plastered all over the headlines.

This book is about the 2%.

# ONE

Smack! The impact stung Emil's hand.

*I can't believe I forgot to ask the question. Reminder to self: never make this man really mad.*

"Rough day at work, Dad?" Emil pulled the baseball from his glove and tossed it back.

"What?" Francis asked, coming out of his daze.

"You're bringing the heat." Emil smiled and shook his glove for emphasis.

"I'm sorry, boy." He lobbed the ball back to Emil. "I've just got a lot on my mind."

*That's never good. If he's got a lot on his mind, then it wasn't a good day. And if it wasn't a good day, then it won't be a good evening.*

"It's OK." Emil smiled. "I don't mind."

Francis couldn't help but smile too.

*How is he always so upbeat? He's so positive it's just infectious. Nothing ever gets him down.*

Emil threw the ball back much harder making his father's glove smack. Francis grinned a little broader.

"And that was?"

"Just a little payback." Emil gave a sly grin.

*Let's see if he can handle this.*

1

Francis reached way back, looking like he was going to throw a major-league fastball. Emil braced for it, but instead Francis threw a curveball that he was unprepared for. It bounced off his glove and rolled away, with Emil in hot pursuit.

"Just remember, son," Francis said as Emil retrieved the ball, "when you think you've got life figured out, that's when it usually throws you a nasty curve."

Emil shook his head.

*Dad loves to give me these object lessons.*

"I think I'm done for the day."

"Why?" Emil frowned.

"I don't want this to escalate until someone gets hurt." Francis paused. "If you end up with a black eye or something, your mother'll skin me alive."

They turned and started toward the small, two-bedroom house they called home.

"Dad," Emil asked, walking through grass that desperately needed mowing, "why do we live so far from your job?"

*Because I hate Larsan and don't want my family anywhere near that city.*

"No reason. Why? Don't you like riding the bus forty minutes to school?"

"No, that's my favorite part of the day, goofing off with my buddies. Well, my second favorite. My favorite time is when you come home from work."

"That's my favorite time too." Francis smiled.

"If you've had a good day."

"Meaning what?"

"Well, I learned a long time ago to ask you how your day was as soon as you walk in the door," Emil said. "If you say 'fine,' 'good,' or even 'tolerable,' I know it's going to be a good evening. If you say 'bad' or 'I don't want to talk about it,' I just go to my room and put on my headphones to drown out the noise of the inevitable fight."

*How old is this kid? His mother could learn a thing or two from him*, Francis thought.

"Unfortunately, I work in a very stressful job," he said. "Am I really that bad?"

"Sometimes." Emil paused. "Other times you just need to be left alone to de-stress."

"How'd you get so smart?"

"I learned from you."

Francis wrapped his arm around Emil's shoulders, and they walked in silence.

*When did he get so tall?*

"Dad, do you ever get tired of taking care of bad people?"

"Not everyone in prison is a bad person, son," Francis said. "Some of them have just made bad choices."

Emil nodded.

"But yes, sometimes I do get tired of taking care of ungrateful, bad people."

"Will it ever stop?" Emil raised his eyebrows. "Will people ever stop being bad?"

"Only if we make them, son."

The haunted look in Francis' eye made Emil shudder.

# TWO

Heads up, guys," Phil said. "Here comes Harley."

"There's the best case for birth control I've ever heard," Glenn muttered.

"Maybe he's just had a hard life," Emil said.

"I heard his mom beats him every day," Phil said.

"Yeah, well, it's not enough," Glenn said.

Harley marched down the hallway like he owned Frost Creek Middle School. Anyone who stood in his way got shoved into a locker.

"Watch it!" Harley said, slamming Emil into a wall.

Emil whipped around to face Harley.

"You got something to say?"

*Calm down, he's just trying to pick a fight. Ignore him.*

"I'm talking to you, fat boy."

*Don't do it. Don't fall for it.* Emil started to walk away.

Harley grabbed Emil and spun him around to face him. They stared each other down. Harley drew back his fist just as Mr. Terog came out of his science class.

"What's going on here?" the teacher demanded.

"Nothing," Harley said, letting go of Emil.

"Get to class," Mr. Terog said.

4

"I'll see you later," Harley told Emil, and then he stalked away.

Glenn was excited as they walked to class. "You can take him," he said.

"Take who where?" Emil frowned.

"Harley—you can beat him," Glenn said.

"Are you nuts?" Phil said. "Harley'll tear him up and throw him in the trash."

"But they're nearly the same size, and Harley's never been challenged before," said Glenn.

"He hasn't been challenged now," Emil said.

"You're kidding, right?" Glenn asked. "You stood toe-to-toe with the biggest bully in school, and you think he's just gonna let that go?"

The bell rang, and the boys went into their last class of the day. When the final bell rang, they all went to the bus. Phil and Glenn got on the bus without noticing that Emil wasn't behind them.

As Harley boarded the bus with a grin, Phil glanced behind him. "Emil was right behind me," he said.

The bus started to back out.

"Wait!" Glenn yelled, waving at the bus driver. "Emil's not here yet."

Just then, Emil stumbled onto the bus.

"Oh, my God," bus driver said. His eyes grew round seeing Emil covered with scratches and blood. "What happened to you?"

"I fell down some stairs," Emil lied.

"Yeah," Glenn whispered, "some stairs named *Harley*. I can't believe Emil's going to let him get away with beating him like that."

"You okay, bud?" Phil said.

"I'll live." Emil said.

"Not for long once your dad sees you. It looks like you were trampled by a herd of cattle."

"I'll live," Emil said with moisture forming in the corners of his eyes.

"I hope so." Phil said.

~

When Emil got home, his mother stared at him, her eyebrows knit in annoyance. She grabbed his ear.

"Don't you dare bleed on my rug," she squealed. "And look what you've done to your new shirt. I should give you a beating myself. Where do you think the money comes from to buy you new clothes? Your father works hard in that hellhole and this is how you repay him? Get out of my sight. Go get cleaned up."

*Thanks, Mom.*

Ten minutes and one quick change later Emil's dad walked in the door.

*There's Dad, right on time. Do I hide? Do I lie to him? Neither of those will turn out well for me when he finds out the truth. Oh well, I better get downstairs and greet him or he'll know something's wrong.*

He approached his father with a smile. "Hey, Dad, how was your day?"

"Pretty good." Francis did a double take at seeing the scratches and bruises on Emil. "Looks like I should ask how *your* day was. What happened to you?"

*Tell the truth or he'll be pissed.*

"Well?" Dad said.

"I got beat up by a bully."

"What? Did you tell anyone about it?"

"No."

"Why not?"

"It happened right before I left school, and the kid rides my bus. I couldn't tell anyone without him seeing."

"Who was it?"

"Harley Richardson."

"That figures," he said. "Those Richardsons are a bad lot. Tell you what, after supper I'll teach you some defensive moves."

"So you want me to fight him?"

"I want you to be able to stand up for yourself," Francis said. "I won't be around forever to fight your battles for you. If you let someone else rule you through fear, you'll be a slave to that fear until you stand up and face them."

Emil saw the haunted look in his father's eye and it made him shudder.

"No, you're not," Rosemarie said, coming in from the kitchen. "You're not going to teach our son to be a thug."

"It's just some self-defense moves he needs to know."

"I forbid it."

"Not this time," Francis said with quiet forcefulness.

Rosemarie turned and stomped to the kitchen muttering Mexican curses, and slammed the door behind her.

The silence hung like a stormcloud waiting to burst as they ate.

After supper, Rosemarie cleared the table and muttered as Francis and Emil moved the furniture in the living room to one side to make space. She glanced into the living room, then trudged to the kitchen to do the dishes.

"I'll show you some moves that have kept me out of the hospital more than a few times, even saved my life," Francis said.

"Is your job really that dangerous?"

"Not if you know how to handle yourself," Francis lied.

Francis went over basic defensive moves, holds and pressure points. Emil picked up the basics with ease, but the rest gave him a little trouble. They practiced over and over for hours until Emil got the hang of each move.

Around midnight, Francis announced, "I'm tired. I'm going to bed."

He took three steps, then turned around and charged at

Emil. Emil didn't think; he reacted. He sidestepped the charge, threw his leg out, grabbed his father's arm with one hand, and pushed him to the floor with the other. Francis landed with a heavy thud that knocked the wind out of him.

Rosemarie came running into the room.

"What was that?" she exclaimed, expecting to see Emil lying on the floor, bleeding. Instead, she found Francis lying on his back unable to speak.

Emil was kneeling beside him. "I'm sorry, Dad," he said over and over.

After a minute Francis sat up, turned to Emil, and said, "That's OK, boy. You did good."

"Look at this room!" Rosemarie said. "It looks like a bulldozer plowed through it and smells like old sweat socks. I want every stick of furniture back where it was before either of you go to bed, or so help me!"

"It's OK, Mom," Emil said quickly. "We'll put it all back."

Rosemarie stormed from the room, muttering in Spanish. Emil and his dad looked at each other and then erupted with laughter. They smiled and chuckled the whole time they were moving the furniture back.

"Good job, son," Francis said. "I think you'll be all right."

"Thanks, Dad. I hope I didn't hurt you too bad."

Emil smiled.

Francis smiled back.

"That's the most fun I've ever had while taking a beating." He tousled Emil's hair. "Good night, son."

# THREE

Emil yawned and stretched while getting out of bed and looking at the clock.

*Oh good. It's only seven o'clock.*

"Seven o'clock? I'm late!"

He rushed downstairs.

*I need to thank Dad before he leaves.*

"Your father already left for work," Rosemarie said. "He wanted to wake you early, but I wouldn't let him."

Emil's face fell.

"I wish you would've," Emil mumbled.

"What's that?" she asked, raising an eyebrow.

Emil knew that look. It usually preceeded plate or cup when her and Francis argued.

"Nothing; gotta go get ready. I don't wanna miss the bus."

"Don't go getting into any fights," she called after him.

He didn't hear her. He was too busy drinking in the beautiful spring day—the smell of flowers and freshly mowed grass, the heavy air, dew on the leaves, birds chirping—all the sights, sounds, and smells that fear had stolen from him. That fear rose up again as the yellow metal beast hurtled toward him.

For a moment, he considered turning and running back to the house. But that would only incur the wrath of his mother.

*I have to face this, head-on.*

He straightened his shoulders as the bus stopped. He mounted the stairs and walked straight back to Harley. "You ready for round two?" he asked.

"Anytime, punk."

"Today, lunchtime, behind the school gymnasium."

Harley smiled. "I'll add a few more bruises to your collection."

"Just be there." Emil turned and walked four rows up to his seat.

Glenn and Phil stared at him in disbelief. Emil could feel their eyes boring into him.

*Can they see me shaking?*

Emil tried everything he could to keep himself calm as they arrived at school.

He walked to his locker and stood there, motionless.

*So this is what a death sentence feels like.*

"What's wrong?" Phil said from three lockers down. "Did you forget your combination?"

"No."

"Are you thinking about how stupid it was to challenge Harley like that?"

"No," Emil lied as his quivering hand turned the dial of his lock.

Phil shook his head.

"Good luck with that denial."

Then they walked to class.

Emil couldn't think of anything other than watching the clock during his classes.

*It's ticking down to my execution. Maybe the governor will call and commute my sentence.*

The ludicrous thought made him smile for the first time.

Some of the tension seemed to bleed away through the smile.

Lunchtime came. Emil and his buddies made their way behind the gym only to find a lot more people than they expected. Dozens of kids who had fallen victim to Harley's beatings were standing around waiting. When they saw Emil, they started to cheer.

"E-mil, E-mil, E-mil!"

As encouraging as the cheers were to Emil, they enraged Harley. He stood in the corner, pounding his fist into his palm as he glared at Emil.

Emil waded through the crowd and found Harley.

"Needed an audience to watch you get stomped?" Harley asked.

"Maybe all the people you pounded would like a chance at some payback," Emil smiled.

"Are we gonna fight, or are you trying to bore me to death?"

"Whenever you're ready."

Instantly, Harley launched himself at Emil, but Emil sidestepped the charge and drove his elbow into the back of Harley's skull. Harley collapsed in a heap. He lay there for a moment, stunned, then staggered back to his feet, rage pulsing in his temples. He shook his head, trying to clear the cobwebs, then fixed his eyes on Emil. He lumbered up to him and threw a wild haymaker. Emil ducked, then threw a couterpunch into Harley's exposed armpit, hitting a nerve cluster.

Harley reeled and held his right arm over his ribs to cover the pain. He charged again and this time managed to catch Emil in a bear hug. He started to squeeze. Emil's ribs were screaming for him to get free when he shoved his finger with all his might into a pressure point on Harley's chest right below the neck. Harley screamed and let him go.

Emil fell to his knees, gasping for breath when Harley kicked him in the ribs and then grabbed him by the hair and pulled him up. He wrapped his arms around Emil's neck in a submission hold.

The crowd gasped, seeing Emil fall and their hopes collapse with him.

"Now whatcha gonna do, tough guy?"

Emil started seeing spots. He reached up in desperation, grabbed Harley's thumb, and bent it backward with every ounce of strength he had left. Harley screamed and released him, but Emil didn't let go of his thumb. He drove Harley to his knees in pain.

"Now, say it's over."

"What's over?" Harley asked through gritted teeth.

"This fight, your career as a bully, and any thought you might have of revenge."

Harley paused.

Emil put more pressure on his thumb, bringing Harley to the verge of tears.

"OK, OK, it's over!"

The crowd erupted in thunderous cheers.

Emil let him go and helped him up just as Mr. Terog walked around the corner.

"What's going on here?"

The tumult ended in a heartbeat as the children looked to Emil for the answer.

"Someone's going to tell me, or else."

"We were playing kickball, sir," Emil said. "I just scored the winning run.

Mr. Terog eyed him and Harley warily. "I don't see a ball."

"I kicked it into the weeds. They're still looking for it ... right, Harley?"

"Umm ... right."

The teacher eyed the weeds dubiously.

"Recess is almost over," he said.

"We'll go out and help them look for the ball," Emil said.

Mr. Terog walked away slowly.

As soon as the teacher was out of earshot, Emil said, "Everyone should go back to class and pretend this fight never happened."

They all started walking away, but Emil pulled Harley aside to talk to him.

"Look, I don't know what's happening with you, if it's something at home that's causing it or what, but I think you need to talk to a counselor about it. I'll go with you if you want."

"Why?"

"For moral support."

"No, I mean, why do you care?"

"Because I think you need a friend more than you need abuse or punishment."

Harley eyed him cautiously.

"Whatever. I'll think about it."

"That's all I ask."

# FOUR

It was shift change at Larsan Prison, and Francis Sorn came on duty. The start of his shift was always boring. Watching an inmate clean wasn't the most exciting thing to do, but that was his assignment.

The inmate put every ounce of energy into doing his job. He had mopped the entire tier, taking great pains to clean every inch of floor. He made it look effortless, and the floors shone when he was done. Like a model inmate, he was meticulous about his assigned tasks.

"Morning, Officer Sorn," the inmate said cheerfully while wringing out his mop. "How's the weather today?"

"All clear," Francis said, looking at a window being pelted with rain. "Not a cloud in the sky."

"Excellent. I'm finished mopping. Could you unlock the supply closet for me?"

"Sure," Francis mumbled.

"What's wrong?" The inmate raised his eyebrows. "You don't seem very happy today."

*As if you really care.* The officer just grunted as they arrived at the supply closet. He unlocked the door and entered before the inmate. He checked the room to make sure they were alone.

## Chapter 4

"I'm not very happy!" He grabbed the inmate by the collar and pinned him to the wall. "I'm not happy being your damn drug dealer. I'm not happy playing these stupid games. I'm not happy risking my job and my freedom for a piece of trash like you!"

"But you came to me," the inmate choked out.

Francis paused and loosened his grip.

"I never came to you for anything."

"Sure you did." The inmate smiled. "You were complaining about that bitch of yours spending money you didn't have."

"You roped me into your drug ring."

"I offered you some extra money; you made your own choice."

"I had no choice; my wife was bankrupting us."

"So, I helped you."

"And you got your drugs."

"And you got your money, so what's the problem?"

Francis stared at him in silence. *What would Emil think of his old man if he knew?*

"Did somebody rat you out?"

No response.

The inmate started laughing.

"Did you grow a conscience?"

Francis's blood began to boil. He grabbed the inmate by the neck.

"So, you want out?" the inmate asked, gasping for breath.

"Consider this my two-weeks' notice."

"No problem," the inmate choked and clutched his throat.

Francis eyed him warily and then slowly released him.

"Can I at least have my last shipment?"

"Yeah. It's over there with the pile of rags."

The inmate found several bags of white powder. As

usual, they were tied together to form a belt so he could easily hide them under his clothes.

"All done," he said. "The money will be wired to your account—as usual."

*Just as pretty as you please. Would you like fries with that?* Francis thought bitterly. He nodded and turned to unlock the door. A sharp pain shot through his back and then his chest. He looked down to see a sharpened piece of plastic sticking out of his uniform shirt, which was turning from gray to dark red.

As he collapsed to the floor, the inmate ripped the shank back out and cleaned it off with one of the rags.

"Consider that your severance pay. Nobody quits on me."

Francis opened his mouth to try calling for help, but all that came out was a bloody gurgle.

Without even looking back, the inmate stepped into the hallway. He closed the door and strolled back to his cell whistling a happy tune as he went. Francis Sorn lay in a pool of his own blood for nearly two hours before someone found him. By then it was too late.

# FIVE

Emil Sorn, report to the principal's office," the loudspeaker blared. Emil put his lunch tray on the counter and walked slowly down the hall. He stopped in front of a door that read, **Principal Edwards**, and turned the knob.

"Come in, Mr. Sorn," the principal said with a scowl.

He stepped inside and saw someone else sitting there too.

"Mom?"

She silently stared into his eyes.

*He has his father's eyes.*

Tears streamed down her face. The principal's scowl turned to concern as he looked at her.

"Will you be alright to drive home?"

She nodded.

"You're dismissed, Mr. Sorn. Your mother will explain the circumstances."

Emil followed his mother to the car. It felt like a funeral march.

*What's the big deal? It was just a little fight. She's acting as though I've killed someone. I just need to talk to dad; he'll understand.*

She dabbed her eyes as she drove towards home, then broke into uncontrollable sobs. The car swerved into the other lane, heading straight for another car.

"Mom!" Emil screamed. "What're you doing?"

She seemed like she had lost interest in driving.

"Mom, this isn't funny! Get back over!"

In desperation, Emil grabbed the wheel and yanked it over as hard as he could. The tires screeched in protest as they bit into the road and sent the car careening through their lane and towards the side of the road. They missed the oncoming car by mere inches as the driver swerved away from them and blew his horn.

"Mom, hit the brakes!"

Rosemarie hadn't come out of her daze and they were rapidly approaching a telephone pole. Not knowing what else to do, Emil reached over and slammed the car into park, sending it into a skid. Gravel flew as a dust cloud enveloped the car and Emil prayed.

The car lurched to a stop. Emil looked out his window as the dust cleared and saw the phone pole mere inches away from his door.

"What the hell is wrong with you?" He screamed at her. "Is this your way of punishing me for fighting, by trying to kill me?"

He glared at her with eyes of rage, but they transformed into eyes of concern. She hadn't moved. In fact, she still had her foot on the gas. The engine was revving faster and sounded like it was about to explode. Emil turned the keys to stop the engine and looked at his mother with a little fear.

"Mom, please tell me what's wrong." He reached out with trembling hands and held hers.

"Your father," she said between sobs.

"What about him?"

She composed herself enough to talk.

"He's dead."

"What?"

"He was killed today, by an inmate."

"What? No. He'll be home in a few hours."

"Emil ... " she said softly, "he's not coming home."

He sat there staring out through the windshield, not moving.

"Emil?" she said.

"You're lying. This is some sort of trick to make me feel bad about fighting today."

"You really think I would pretend your father was dead just to make you feel bad?"

Emil's answer was a withering glare. He tried to open his door but it banged against the pole and would only open a few inches. He crawled over the seat, opened the back door and got out.

"What're you doing?" She called after him as he started walking. "Get back in this car."

He didn't answer. He didn't pause. He just kept walking.

*It can't be true. How can she do something like this? Wait til I tell dad she almost wrecked the car and I had to save us. There's gonna be a lot of yelling in the house tonight.*

The last thought made him smile.

*I'm not afraid of her. I'm proud of standing up to that bully today. Somebody needed to do it and I stepped up. Dad will be proud of me too. Why does she have to ruin everything?*

"Emil Francis Sorn, you get back in this car this instant!"

He didn't pause, turn, or break his stride.

Rosemarie's anger at Emil had helped her regain her composure. She followed him on the side of the road in the car. They traveled this way for nearly a mile, looking every bit like the world's smallest parade, until they reached home.

Emil ran inside.

"Dad! Dad, you'll never guessed what happened today."

He ran from room to room, searching in vain. He scoured the house from the attic to the basement, even searching their tiny backyard with no sign of his father.

Doubt had begun to creep into his mind. According to the clock his father should've been home half an hour ago. Little facts began nagging him now. His father's car wasn't in the garage or parked in the driveway. There was no empty lunchbox sitting on the kitchen table.

*I know it's a trick. He probably had to work overtime and she's trying to upset me. He is gonna be so pissed when he finds out what she did.*

An evil grin spread across Emil's face. He looked over at the phone hanging on the wall in the kitchen. He picked up the receiver and dialed the number that was written on a faded piece of paper taped to the wall.

Rosemarie came in the front door and saw Emil on the phone.

"Who are you calling?"

"Larsan State Prison," came a voice of the other end of the line.

"Yes, could I speak to Officer Sorn please?" Emil said.

"Umm … just a minute."

Emil expected his mother to rip the phone from his hand, but she didn't. She didn't protest either. She just stood there, watching him. That frightened him more than anything.

"Lieutenant Wright, how can I help you?"

"Yes, I'd like to speak with officer Sorn if I could, please."

"Officer Sorn?"

"Yes, sir."

"Who is this?"

"This is his son, Emil."

"Hasn't anyone told you yet?"

"Told me what?"

"I'm sorry to have to tell you this, but your father was involved in an incident."

Emil swallowed hard.

"I-is he okay?"

"Son, your father was killed today."

The phone hit the floor, followed closely by Emil. He sat, leaning against the wall, staring at nothing.

Rosemarie picked up the phone and hung it up without saying a word.

"Now do you believe me?" She asked Emil.

He didn't answer, didn't move, didn't blink.

~

He sat there, motionless for hours, staring at the front door. She offered him food and drink, but received no response. A few friends and neighbors straggled through, wishing them condolences. Emil never moved or spoke.

As darkness fell the trickle of well-wishers dried up and Rosemarie sat beside her son trying to comfort him.

"He's really not coming home, you know," she said.

Emil didn't respond.

"OK," she said. "I'm going to bed. You can sleep here if you want, but he won't be walking through that door no matter how long you watch."

Emil didn't move.

She sighed, staring into his empty eyes. The weight of the world crashed down on her. At that moment, she felt more alone than any other time in her life. Tears welled up in her eyes as she struggled to stand. She looked down at her catatonic son, realizing how much he looked like his father, and couldn't take it anymore. She stumbled to her room and collapsed on the bed. She stared over at Francis' empty side of the bed and fell into a tearful sleep.

Emil drifted off to sleep shortly after she left. When he woke, it was almost sunrise. He struggled to his feet, stretching the stiffness out of his body, then ran outside and looked around, but his dad's car wasn't in the driveway. He walked to the end of the drive thinking maybe his dad had parked in the street. He ignored the fact that in his twelve years on Earth he had never once seen his father park on the street.

He reached the sidewalk and looked both directions, but his father's car was nowhere to be found. Slowly, it began to sink in. He turned and started back toward the house when something caught his eye.

He walked into the yard, bent down, and picked up his father's baseball glove. He stared at it for a long time. He could almost picture his dad standing in this very spot just two days ago, throwing the ball to him. Emil collapsed to the dew-covered ground and began to sob. His face, hidden in the glove, made the inside as wet as the outside.

*Why, Dad, why?*

# SIX

Emil didn't go to school for three days. A few family members and friends attended the funeral, including the warden and a couple of officers from Larsan Prison.

As they approached, Rosemarie tried to ignore them.

"I'm so sorry for your loss," the warden said. "Francis was a fine officer."

Rosemarie pretended not to hear him. The warden took the hint and reached down to shake Emil's hand.

"Your dad was a good man," he said. "Don't ever forget that."

"So good that you let him die?" Rosemarie muttered.

"We will find his killer and bring him to justice," the warden said.

"Justice? What the hell do you know about justice? You sit in your office, smoking cigars while good officers like my husband are brutally murdered by scum, and you have the nerve to mention justice to me?"

"This is a very dangerous profession. Francis knew that when he was hired. We deal with the dregs of society, but we do it the best we can. When one of our own gets hurt, we all feel it."

"Oh, please. What do you feel right now? You might be sad for a day or two and then you'll start interviewing to hire his replacement. In less than six months my husband will be reduced to a name on a wall, another statistic that decent people ignore because they don't want to see it. And what will happen to me and my son?"

"I don't know, ma'am."

"You mean you don't care."

"I promise we will find his killer."

"As far as I'm concerned, his killer is standing in front of me," she said.

"I feel the same way," he said, staring into her eyes. "We'll be going now."

She glared daggers into their backs as they walked away. Emil was torn. He wanted to hear about his father from the people who knew him best, but he had no desire to upset his mother.

～

Emil became a shell of a person. On the outside, he appeared normal, but the spark that made him who he was had been dimmed. He barely talked to anyone anymore, especially his mother. Now that it was just he and his mother, Emil began to realize how little they had in common.

He realized how different they were the first time he asked to watch one of his TV shows and she just ignored him. Those first few days gave Emil a taste of what was to come. As soon as he played one of his records in his room she shouted for him to turn that noise off.

～

His mom sent him back to school the day after the funeral.

"I'm sick of seeing you mope around," she told Emil.

When he got on the bus, everyone was silent. No one approached him. No one talked to him. It made him feel even lonelier.

Suddenly, Harley came up and sat beside him. He tensed up waiting for the first blow, physical or verbal, to land. Harley tried to say something to Emil but paused as though struggling to get the words out. Finally, he said, "Real sorry about your dad, man."

Emil wasn't sure what to say, so he just said, "Thanks."

"I lost my mom when I was younger. It took me a long time to get over it."

"Is that why you try to hurt people? Because you got hurt?" Emil asked, knowing he may be treading on thin ice.

"I guess so," Harley said with surprising honesty.

"Did you go see the counselor like I said?"

"Yeah, he told me a lot of useless crap and nearly bored me to sleep."

Emil chuckled.

"It wasn't all that great, huh?"

"I wouldn't say that," Harley said. "The one thing he did do was listen. I don't think I've had anyone listen to my problems for a long time."

"That's good then."

"Yeah."

"Glad I could help."

"Me too," Harley said. "I actually came over here to return the favor."

"OK ... "

"The doc told me how to deal with my mother's death."

Emil swallowed hard, trying to keep the tears from escaping his eyes.

"How?"

"He said your life will never be the same, so don't try to make it the same. You need to find a new normal and go from there."

Emil couldn't trust himself to say anything without breaking down and crying. He merely nodded.

School made him feel much worse. Everyone treated him like he had the plague. No one talked to him except Phil and Glenn. They weren't themselves either. No one seemed to know what to say. Harley's talk was the highlight of Emil's day.

When he got off the bus, he picked up the mail from their mailbox, looked through it, and saw a letter from an insurance company. He told his mom about it when he got in the house, and she nearly ripped his hand off taking it from him.

She opened it in a frenzy, throwing the letter on the table, looking only for the check. When she read the amount, her face dropped. She fell into the chair, still staring at the check. She dropped it and picked up the letter, quickly reading it.

Emil picked up the check and said, "Wow, thirty thousand dollars!"

"Don't touch that!" She squealed, yanking it away from him. When she did, it ripped.

"No," she shrieked, and then she slapped him across the face so hard that it knocked him to the floor.

"Look what you've done!"

She picked up the loose pieces of the check, lumbered past him, and taped it together.

"You're lucky," she hissed, shaking her finger at the stunned boy on the floor. Emil cringed, afraid she might hit him again. Instead, she turned on her heel and stormed out. A moment later he heard the car roar out of the driveway.

He struggled to his feet, shaking, and stumbled to the bathroom. An angry patch of red graced his cheek looking like it may bruise. He opened the medicine cabinet searching for something to take the sting away when his eyes settled on his father's straight razor. He picked it up, opened it, and stared at his reflection in the shining blade. He thought back to a time not so long ago.

~

*Francis drew the razor slowly up his neck, scraping the shaving cream off as he went.*

*"Doesn't that hurt?" Emil said.*

*"Not if you do it right."*

*Emil watched, fascinated.*

*"When can I learn to do that?"*

*Francis chuckled.*

*"Not for a while yet. You don't have anything to shave."*

*Emil jumped up to the mirror to look at his chin. When he did, he accidentally bumped his father's arm causing him to cut himself.*

*"I'm so sorry, dad."*

*Francis wiped away the blood and put a small Band-Aid over it.*

*"It's okay. See, good as new. You need to learn though to be careful with dangerous things."*

*"Is that dangerous?"*

*"Absolutely." Francis said, resuming his shave. "You could hurt or even kill someone with one of these."*

*"Then why do you use it?"*

*"Dangerous things can be controlled as long as you respect them."*

*Francis finished, wiped the remaining shaving cream away, and turned toward Emil.*

*"How do I look?"*

*Emil smiled and gave him two thumbs up.*

*Francis smiled back and mussed his hair.*

~

Emil stared at the razor in his hand and looked in the mirror to see if he had any hairs growing on his chin yet.

Sadness crept over him as he glanced from the razor to his wrist. He brought the blade down and rested it flat on his skin. It felt cool and inviting. He slid the blade along his wrist with the sharp edge trailing behind.

*It doesn't feel any different from a butter knife.*

He stopped the blade and was about to slide it the other way when he heard a door slam.

He quickly put the razor back in the cabinet and went to his room, not wanting to talk to his mother.

# SEVEN

It was a clear, sunny day, but still quite cold. Emil zipped up his worn-out jacket as soon as he stepped off the school bus. It had only been a little over a year since his father had passed away, but to Emil it seemed much longer.

He picked up the mail, as usual. It consisted of bills and past-due notices. He walked in the house, which wasn't much warmer than outside, and set down his backpack, which was falling apart. He had tried to sew it together, and it had worked for a while, but now it needed sewing again. He didn't dare ask for a new one. The last time he tried, his mom went ballistic on him, saying that she barely had enough money to feed him.

*To hear her say it you'd think I was a human garbage can.*

At thirteen years old, Emil had lost thirty pounds in the past year. She barely fed him at all. Emil didn't complain, though. He knew how tight money was and tried to help as much as he could.

Any snow shoveling or lawn mowing money he got, he gave to Mom. She would greedily snatch the money from him and then complain because it wasn't more.

Emil sighed heavily, knowing exactly what he was about to see as he entered the kitchen.

His mother was at the kitchen table, sitting a little too straight. Her hands were folded together, and there was a small residue of silver powder on the table that looked like it had been hastily wiped away. Emil stifled a grin.

*She looks like a little kid who's been caught with her hand in the cookie jar.*

"Did you win anything this time?"

He was answered by her best, 'What do you mean?' look. He went to the trash can and pulled out five scratch-off lottery tickets. She quickly snatched them out of his hand.

"This is none of your business," she snarled at him, then stomped off slamming her bedroom door. Emil laid the bills down on the table, got the sewing kit from the utility drawer and sat on the creaky couch. There was no TV to watch and no radio to listen to—they had been sold long ago. Emil sewed in silence.

The years went by slowly for Emil and his mom. The older he got, the better paying his jobs became. Rosemarie finally stopped thinking that a financial miracle was going to save them and got a job as a waitress. Eventually they caught up on the bills and even managed a luxury or two.

Not that either of them had much time to enjoy the secondhand, black-and-white TV they bought from the Goodwill store, but the coffee pot came in handy. Between school and work, they didn't see each other much, and neither was terribly sad about that.

Emil somehow managed passing grades, but nothing that would land him on the honor roll. It was pretty tough when he was working nearly every evening.

Occasionally he would still go out with his friends, which now included Harley, but it made his mom angry. She never wanted him to spend any money, even what he had earned, but Emil had stashed a little money here and there for himself.

## CHAPTER 7

Eventually, Emil was a senior and thinking about college. He knew what he wanted to do, but he also knew the reaction it would cause at home. He could hear his mother now, 'We don't have money to waste on something as stupid as college.' Of course, she had no idea that he had managed to squirrel away nearly four thousand dollars. If she did, she would steal it from him in a heartbeat.

Finally, the dreaded day came. Emil knew he could no longer put it off; he would have to discuss college with his mother.

She worked late that night, but Emil waited up for her. Around eleven thirty, she trudged through the door. Emil had just finished watching the news when Rosemarie collapsed onto the couch.

"How was your day?" Emil asked.

She raised her head, and gave him a, 'How does it look like my day was?' expression and then let her head fall back against the couch.

"OK ... um ... we need to talk," Emil said.

Every time he uttered those words, she headed for the bedroom. As if avoiding a problem somehow magically made it go away.

This time he was ready. Before she got halfway to her room, he blurted out, "I want to go to college."

She turned and opened her mouth, but before she could protest, Emil said. "I'm already looking into grants to help with tuition and books."

She closed her mouth, thought for a moment, and opened it again. Again, Emil beat her to it.

"And I would start Larsan Community College, so I wouldn't have any housing costs. And I would get a third job, to offset the cost."

Rosemarie regarded Emil.

*Just as stubborn as his father.*

"We don't have money to waste on something as stupid

as college." she said and started to walk away.

"I'll study to be a lawyer!" he called to her as she was reaching for her doorknob.

She froze.

*A lawyer?*

Emil thought he could see actual dollar signs in her eyes when she turned and said, "Okay."

# EIGHT

College was a different animal from high school. Emil applied for every grant known. He qualified for some, but by the time he got his paperwork in, only a few were left. He ended up paying for it mostly out of his own pocket and student loans.

Emil's college days went quickly. Between working two jobs and having four classes a week, not to mention studying and schoolwork, college was a caffeine-fueled blur. The only thing Emil really remembered about it was his criminal-justice professor, who had some radical ideas and who unknowingly planted a seed in Emil's mind.

After two years, Emil earned his associates degree in criminal justice. It was all he was really going for, but he kept that a carefully guarded secret.

*Mom would have two heart attacks if she every found out that I have no intention of becoming a lawyer.*

He told his mother that he wanted to look for a higher-paying job so he could quit his part-time job and have more time to study. Thinking of the pot of gold at the end of the college rainbow, she agreed. He never told her that the job was at Larsan State Prison.

~

"What do you think of our latest batch of applicants?" Deputy Warden Roose asked. Warden Tanzey threw the folders on his desk in disgust.

"I could find better people at a fast-food joint," he replied. "The only one that even remotely impressed me was this Emil Sorn," Roose said, rummaging through the files until he found a certain one.

"Emil Juan Sorn, born June eighteen, 1964, blah, blah, blah, German-Irish-Mexican descent. Wow, that's quite a combination. Graduated from a local college with an associates degree in criminal justice but didn't pursue law school. He's six feet five, one hundred eighty-seven pounds. We'll have to add some meat to this boy. How did his interview go?"

"This kid is idealistic as hell. He says the justice system is too soft on inmates."

"I agree, don't you?"

"Yeah, I do, but I've worked in a prison for a lot of years. I just think this kid is too young to be this jaded. We'll have to keep an eye on him, make sure he doesn't go too far over the edge."

"What makes you say that?"

"I don't know, just the way he looked when I was talking about justice. Like there was something just below the surface screaming to get out."

"Well then, keep an eye on him."

"So, he's hired?"

"Yeah, I'll call him and break the bad news. 'Congratulations, you've just been hired by the worst prison in the state.'"

"That's a helluva thing for the warden to say." Roose laughed.

## CHAPTER 8

A pensive, melancholy shadow passed over Tanzey's face.

"If only it weren't true," he said, looking at Sorn's file.

~

"Thank you very much, warden. I'll see you first thing on Monday."

Emil hung up the phone as a ballistic missile of anger known as Rosemarie shoved a finger in his face.

"No! I absolutely refuse," Emil's mother declared.

"This is what I want to do."

"I won't allow it!"

"You won't allow it?" Emil slowly repeated, as a cauldron of emotions started to bubble.

"I won't let you throw away your life … like …"

"Like? Like Dad threw away his? That's what you want to say, isn't it?"

She stood silently, somewhere between anger and despair.

"Did you love Dad?"

She stared at him with shock in her eyes. "How can you ask me a question like that?"

"Every time I mention him, you change the subject, and when I want to follow in his footsteps, you 'absolutely refuse.'"

"Follow in his footsteps? Right to the grave?"

"I want to honor his memory … unlike you."

It was too much for her.

"You didn't know what your father was! You didn't see what that place had made him. You saw a loving father; you didn't see the drugs, the drinking, the abuse."

"Oh, I've seen my share of abuse," he said, glaring at her.

Rosemarie was shocked by the confrontation.

"I've provided a home for you in your darkest years, and this is how you repay me?"

"The only reason the years were dark is because of you. You stole my childhood. I became your slave. You stole money from me, pretending it was for both of us. Repay you? I already paid for all of this and then some!"

"Your father was a drug dealer. That's why he died."

"You're lying," Emil said with quiet menace.

"Am I? Or did you just see what you wanted to see and ignore the rest?"

The cauldron boiled over. Emil's hand lashed out in a savage backhand across his mother's face. The physical impact knocked her backward at the same time the mental impact sent him reeling.

He stared at his hand, eyes and mouth wide, as though it belonged to someone else. Until that moment, he had never imagined striking his mother. She regained her composure and rubbed her stinging cheek.

"This feels familiar," she said. "This is how my arguments with your father usually ended."

She closed her bedroom door behind her.

# NINE

The powder exploded with a roar that reverberated off the concrete block walls, sending buckshot down the barrel to its intended destination—Anthony Morrilli's chest.

The vicious gang leader looked down in shock at the expanding red stain in the middle of his inmate uniform.

*I can't believe the kid actually had the balls to do it.*

The thought died with him as he toppled over, like a redwood that's been cut down in its prime. His body hit the concrete floor with a hollow thud, splattering blood and spreading silence like the chill of an arctic wind.

Emil Sorn looked down the barrel of the shotgun hardly believing it himself. He knew all eyes were on him, and even though he wanted to go somewhere and throw up, a show of strength was needed. He slowly, deliberately, cycled another round into the chamber, silently daring anyone else to get within fifteen feet of the door he was guarding. The riot came to an abrupt end.

~

An hour later, Emil sat in the warden's office, trying his best not to let the man see his hands shaking.

"All right, kid, what happened?" Warden Tanzey asked, pacing his office floor, puffing on a cigar.

"Well, sir, Mr. Roose met me at the front door, got me a uniform, and started me on a tour. I had never been inside a prison before and didn't know how loud it could get. Mr. Roose took me to where the riot was, and a sergeant gave me a shotgun, telling me, 'Any inmate who gets within fifteen feet of that door, you shoot them right here.' Then he punched me in the middle of the chest."

Tanzey looked at him in disbelief.

"You shot the leader of the worst gang in this prison because he got too close to a door?"

"Yes, sir. Wasn't I supposed to?"

Tanzey looked at Emil with appraising eyes. When he hired the kid, he wasn't sure if he would work out or not, but not in his wildest nightmare did he think that his deputy warden would take him to an active riot scene or that a senior sergeant would hand him a shotgun and say, "guard that door," on his first day. The biggest surprise was that the kid did it.

*I can't believe he shot Morrilli without question, without hesitation. Apparently, there's more to this kid than I thought.*

"Write me a report on exactly what happened, then go home," Tanzey said. "Be back first thing tomorrow. I need to straighten some things out."

After he finished the report, Emil barely remembered driving home. His mind was a blur as a thousand thoughts raced around his head. He tried to slow them down by replaying the day's events.

He was driving to his first day at his new job. He crested a hill, and there it was, Larsan State Prison.

*It looks like an old castle.*

He pictured torture chambers and people on the rack screaming, begging for mercy. He pulled up to the open gate, turned into the parking lot, parked, and walked inside. He stared at the walls and ceiling as he walked, nearly walking into the secretary's desk.

"Take it easy, kid," said a larger, older-looking woman. "Are you lost?"

"No, I'm Emil Sorn. I start today."

She appraised him with her eyes, making him feel uncomfortable. She had the look of a hungry dog that had seen a piece of fresh meat.

"And just what are you starting as?" she said, licking her lips.

"Um ... guard."

"Oh, honey, around here we call them *Corrections Officers*," she said. "The inmates call them *guards*. It's actually disrespectful. Don't go letting anyone catch you using the "G" word or things won't go so well for you."

"Thank you," Emil said. "I won't."

"Anytime, sugar," she said with a wink. "I'll call the deputy warden and tell him you're here."

"Thank you ... for everything."

"Let's just say you owe me one," she said with a smile that looked like a predator sizing up its prey.

Emil suppressed a shudder and sat in the waiting area trying not to think about what exactly the "one" was that he owed.

"Good morning. I'm Bill Roose, deputy warden. How do you like the place so far?"

"Great!" Emil answered, with honest enthusiasm.

*Was I ever that green?* Roose wondered.

"Well, let's get you a uniform and show you around."

The secretary watched them go and made a mental note. *Emil Sorn.*

After he was shown a locker and changed into uniform, they started the tour.

"How many inmates are housed here?" Emil asked.

"Around thirteen hundred," Roose answered. "This is an older prison, not nearly as big as they build them nowadays, and this was the last prison designed by Herbert

Holmes, the famous architect. After he retired, they started building the more modern style. Translation, giant cubes of concrete."

"Do you ever have any problems with the inmates?" Emil asked.

*How many kids have I seen just like this one? Fresh out of college, with a criminal-justice degree, who think they know everything but don't have a hint of backbone. What, do these kids come off an assembly line? Are they hatched out of pods?*

He glanced at Emil, who was looking around starry-eyed. A sly grin came across Roose's face.

"Hey, kid, how would you like to see a cellblock?"

"Um ... sure."

Roose was going to enjoy scaring the hell out of this kid. He wasn't sure why, but there was something about him he didn't like. They took a door that led down a long hallway. Emil could almost feel the walls shaking, and he heard a dull roar.

"What's that?" Emil asked.

Roose just smiled and kept walking. The roar got louder as they approached the end of the hall. When they opened the door, Emil was nearly knocked backward by the deafening noise. He looked up to see hundreds of inmates all screaming, cursing, banging on their cell doors, making an incredible racket. A handful of officers in riot gear stood in the middle of the room. Emil noticed some of the cell doors had been damaged and were about to fail. Many more were in the process of failing. The sergeant in charge ran over.

"Is this all you brought?" he yelled, looking at Emil.

"This is Emil Sorn. It's his first day," Roose yelled. "The Emergency Response Team should be on their way."

The sergeant held out a twelve-gauge shotgun to Emil.

"You know how to use one of these, kid?"

"Yes, sir!"

"Good! If anyone in orange gets within fifteen feet of that door, you shoot them right here." He punched Emil in the middle of the chest, knocking him backward a step, and then handed him the shotgun.

"You got it?"

"Yes, sir!"

The sergeant started to walk away when Roose grabbed his arm.

"Are you sure about this?"

The sergeant looked at Emil and then back at Roose.

"You brought him here."

He turned and went back to his men.

"I'm going to check on the ERT. Be safe, kid," Roose said. He sprinted through the door that Emil was now guarding.

Emil held the shotgun in front of his chest and felt a surge of power rush through him. He realized that he held the power of life and death in his hands. A small grin appeared on Emil's face. Morrilli got free from the officers and started toward the door Emil was guarding. He saw the shotgun and paused, until he noticed the person holding it looked like a kid. He smiled and strode toward the door. He paused again when the kid aimed the shotgun directly at him.

"You don't wanna do that now, do you?" Morrilli said, making sure the shank in his sleeve was still hidden. Emil gave no warning, just followed his every move while mentally measuring how close he was to the door.

"You couldn't take a life, boy. You don't have it in you. You don't know what it takes," Morrilli said, advancing again. "Why don't you just put that gun down before innocent people get hurt?"

Emil grinned a little broader.

"You're not innocent," Emil said, as Morrilli crossed his invisible line and Emil pulled the trigger.

# TEN

Lunchroom duty was about as boring as it gets in prison. Standing in a corner, watching five hundred inmates eat was bad enough, but doing it while hungry was infinitely worse. This was Emil's third time doing lunchroom. He was behind getting to work today and had to skip breakfast. The beef stroganoff they served for lunch smelled fantastic, probably more due to Emil's hunger than the kitchen staff's actual cooking prowess. As the inmates finished eating, his stomach gave a loud growl, catching the attention of a passing inmate.

"Whoa, son! Last time I heard something growl like that, it was chasin' an antelope. Sounds like you need to get some grub in that belly. Ya already look like a stiff breeze would blow you down."

The inmate chuckled, and Emil couldn't help but crack a smile.

"I'm Frank Carson, son, and if any of these boys give you any trouble, you just let me know."

Emil nodded as Frank checked out his name tag.

"Sorn? Any relation to Francis Sorn?"

"Maybe."

Frank looked into his eyes.

## CHAPTER 18

"You're his boy, ain't ya?"

"Maybe."

"C'mon, son, there ain't no secrets in prison."

Emil sighed.

"Yeah, he was my dad."

"Real sorry 'bout what happened to him. He was a good officer, one of the best."

"Thanks."

"Well, I won't keep ya from watching these 'dangerous criminals.' You 'member what I said."

Emil grunted and turned his eyes back to the lunchroom, but Carson's words haunted his thoughts. He had tried asking the veteran officers about his father. He couldn't get a straight answer. In desperation, he sought out Frank Carson.

"It took ya a week of asking around before you came back to me? Yeah, I knew your dad; he was a good officer."

"Everyone's been saying that, but no one will tell me what happened."

"Are ya sure ya want to hear the truth? "I'll warn ya, it ain't gonna be a pretty picture."

"I have to know."

"Well, it all started around the time you were born. Francis just wasn't makin' enough money to make ends meet. He was approached about bringing in some extra cigarettes to help inmates between commissary orders. At first, he wouldn't do it, but I guess his bills got out of hand. I think there was some problem with his wife too, maybe gambling. Eventually he agreed to do it. He made a little side money, and no one was the wiser."

Emil gritted his teeth.

"I thought you said he was a good officer."

"He was. He just needed a little extra money."

Steeling himself, Emil remembered how much he wanted to know the real story.

"How long did this go on?"

"Years. Until someone wanted him to bring in something stronger."

"Drugs?" Emil asked, wondering how long he could contain himself.

"Just uppers and downers at first. He didn't like it, but he was already in too deep."

"In too deep?"

"He tried to say that he wouldn't do it, but the inmate who controlled him threatened to get him fired if he didn't keep bringing it in."

"Threatened him?"

"That's how it works, kid. They pull you in so deep that you can't get out."

"Who was it? Who threatened my father?" Emil demanded.

"Err ... someone with a lot of time to do."

"Is he still here?"

"Look, kid, you don't wanna go lookin' for trouble, there's plenty of trouble here without lookin' for more."

"Is ... he ... still ... here?" Emil said, barely containing himself.

Frank sighed. "Yes."

"Who is he?"

"I can't tell you that."

"Tell me."

"You're too upset about this right now. We'll talk about it later."

"Tell me!"

"No. And if you keep acting like this, I won't tell you any more, ever."

Emil realized how close he was to the truth. It was driving him like a carrot dangling just out of a donkey's reach.

"I'm sorry," Emil said, composing himself. "I would like

to finish this conversation at another time. If you'll excuse me, I have to finish my rounds."

"Thank you for stopping by," Frank said. "I enjoyed our talk."

"I did too," Emil said. Then he slowly walked away.

# ELEVEN

Emil tried for days to confirm the story Frank had told him, but he kept getting stonewalled. Some people let little clues slip, suggesting that the story was accurate. Emil paid Frank another visit.

"You back to hear some more?"

"Yes. I've settled down, and I think I can handle it."

"You best be real cool, because this next part ain't pleasant."

"I'm ready."

"Well, soon bigger demands were being made of your dad. He was bringing in marijuana, heroin, crack, you name it. This inmate's main supplier delivered to him, and Francis became the main supplier for the prison."

"And no one noticed?"

"Actually, the problem was, they did. The little enterprise got too big, and soon people were asking questions. One thing led to another, and the warden called your dad into his office. He went expecting to get fired, possibly arrested. But instead, the warden wanted a cut, and your dad got put in the best place to distribute the drugs."

"Stop calling it that! Call it contraband.'"

## CHAPTER 11

"OK, contraband," Frank said, rolling his eyes.

"Then what happened?" Emil asked.

"Your dad tried to quit."

"Well, why didn't they just let him and get a new distributor?"

"This ain't Walmart. You can't just up and quit. Francis knew too much about many of the wrong sort of people."

"In other words, they killed him to silence him?"

"That's the way things work. Somebody tries to get one over on you, tries to destroy what you've taken years to build; there needs to be a response."

"A response? Murder is *a response* now?"

"I've found it sends the loudest message. It's a message that people don't ignore."

"My father was killed as a message," Emil said slowly, letting the thought sink in.

"Yes, and now I can continue my dealings with the Sorn family."

"What do you mean, *dealings?*"

"Haven't you figured it out yet, kid? I'm the one who controlled your father."

Emil's face flushed. "What?"

"That's right. And when I couldn't control him, I killed him. And now I'm the one who's gonna control you."

"That's not gonna happen." Emil said through gritted teeth.

"You may want to reconsider when I report that you've been in my cell threatening me."

"I haven't done that!"

"You and I know that, but no one else does."

"An officer's word is better than an inmate's," Emil said, with his head held high.

Frank laughed.

"Wow! You are green. You've been here, what? Two months? I've been here twenty-seven years; I'm a trustee.

They'll believe ol' Uncle Frank over some snot-nosed rookie."

"What if I refuse?"

"That's easy, I put a hit out on you."

"Why?"

"Because I've already told you too much, and hitting someone in here is easy and cheap. A lot easier than answering a bunch of questions."

"Let me think about it."

"Why? So you can go blabbing? I don't think so. Yes or no, right now!"

"Then the answer is no!"

"How disappointing. I thought family counted for something. You could've continued your father's legacy," Frank said with a sneer. "Oh well, I killed one Sorn, I might as well make it two."

Emil was shaking with rage. It was too much for him to stand. He dove into Frank, fists flying, raining blows down on him. It was the last thing Frank expected. His shock gave Emil the upper hand, briefly. Frank outweighed Emil by a good eighty pounds, and although he had a belly, it was mostly muscle. He worked out five days a week and could bench three hundred and fifty pounds without breaking a sweat. Emil's surprise attack was short lived once Frank got hold of him. Although Emil had landed many punches, they didn't have much power behind them. All they really managed to do was infuriate Frank and alert other inmates that a fight was in progress. A crowd formed outside Frank's cell, trapping Emil inside.

Frank unleashed a right to his temple that made Emil's knees buckle. While he tried to regain his balance, Frank threw a left that fractured Emil's jaw and knocked him back to the floor.

Momentum had swung, and Frank now held the upper hand. In desperation, he kicked at the nerve cluster on

Frank's inner thigh. Frank was stunned for a moment.

Emil tried to use this time to get back on his feet. He made it as far as his knees before Frank recovered, gave him a savage kick to the ribs. The force of the kick threw him halfway across the cell.

Frank grabbed his shirt and unleashed a flurry of massive blows to Emil's head and chest. Blood flew with every punch. Emil's resistance was gone. All he could do was lie there and wait for the inevitable. His vision started to get hazy. He could hear someone talking, but they sounded like they were at the end of a long tunnel.

"Your father was a lot tougher than you." Frank said, as he hovered over a barely conscious Emil.

He pulled a shank from under his pillow. His lips drew back into a feral grin as he held it over his blood-covered head.

*He looks like some deranged pagan priest about to make a sacrifice.*

As he faded into unconsciousness, he heard the sound of Frank screaming. Then everything went black.

# TWELVE

Darkness.

*Beep, beep, beep.*

Emil yawned. "Time for another day of babysitting."

*Beep, beep, beep.*

"All right, I'm up. Somebody shut that alarm off."

*Beep, beep, beep.*

"I said I'm up."

It kept beeping.

"I'm gonna smash that alarm clock!" Emil tried to turn it off. "Why won't my arms move?"

*Beep, beep, beep.*

"Are my eyes open?"

A woman in white entered room 415.

"Good morning, Mr. Sorn. Time for your meds," she said as she injected a needle into a tube. "There you go. See you in a few hours."

"Wait!" Emil shouted. "Where am I? Why is it still dark? Who are you?"

But she didn't even pause on her way out of the room.

"What's wrong with me? Why can't I move?"

A few hours later, the doctor entered the room and checked Emil's chart.

Then a young, attractive nurse walked in.

"Good morning, Mr. Sorn. Time to check your vitals."

She ran through a diagnostic procedure she had done thousands of times. "Looking a little better than yesterday. I'll see you later," she said, smiling.

"Why do you do that?" the doctor asked her on her way out.

"Do what?"

"Talk to him."

"Why shouldn't I?"

"Because it has never been proven that comatose patients hear anything or that talking to them does one bit of good."

She looked back at Emil. "You never know." Then she smiled at the doctor and left.

A few hours later, a woman stood outside the door to room 415 for a long moment not sure if she really wanted to see what was behind it. She built up the courage to grab the handle and go inside.

She gasped at the sight of the person lying on the bed with tubes running into and out of his body. Casts and bandages covered him, making him look barely human, let alone like her only son.

She leaned down and read the chart just to be sure.

"Sorn, Emil," it read.

She walked along the side of the bed, tears welling in her eyes. She looked down at the side of his face that was uncovered and slapped him as hard as she could.

His head rolled to the side and then rolled back, like a doll's.

"That's for not listening to me!" she screamed at him. "I told you not to follow in your father's footsteps. Why didn't you listen? Why?"

She collapsed onto his chest and convulsed with wracking sobs.

"It's good to see you too, Mom," Emil thought.

An hour later Warden Tanzey walked into room 415 only to discover a woman slumped over Emil. He hesitated and turned to leave, but his presence was enough to wake her. She looked at him, and her face turned bright red as she composed herself and straightened her hair.

"I'm sorry to disturb you," Tanzey said. "I was checking in on Mr. Sorn."

"Are you a doctor?"

"No, I'm the warden at Larsan State Prison."

Her eyes blazed with sudden fire.

"You're responsible for my son lying here barely clinging to his life."

He fumbled for words for a moment but then regained his composure.

"The inmate who did this was tased and will get attempted murder charges," Tanzey said. "I guarantee you he will never leave that prison."

"It looks like he doesn't need to leave your prison to cause damage," she growled.

"I'm sorry that your son was injured, and I pray for his recovery," Tanzey said. "Rest assured, when he recovers, he will still have a job waiting for him."

"Injured?" she said as though hearing the word for the first time. "I have been injured. You took my husband; I won't let you take my son."

"Who was your husband?" Tanzey said, unprepared for the way this conversation was going.

"Francis Sorn," she said. "He was killed in that hellhole eight years ago."

"I am sorry for your loss, but I've only been warden for five years."

"That doesn't help Emil."

Tanzey knew a hopeless battle when he saw it. He turned to leave.

"It was nice meeting you, Mrs. Sorn. I'll stop in to see your son at another time."

"It was not nice meeting you," she growled. "And don't bother."

Meanwhile, deep inside the recesses of Emil's mind ...

*It was a foggy day. So foggy that Emil was surprised he could even see the baseball to catch it. But somehow where he stood was clear. Emil caught the baseball in his glove.*

*He looked at his dad and smiled, then he threw the ball back to Francis. They tossed the ball back and forth, talking as they did.*

*"I'm guessing things aren't going too well for you, son," Francis said.*

*Emil tried to speak; he wanted to ask a thousand questions, but he didn't know where to start.*

*"It's OK, boy, I did it for you."*

*"What do you mean?"*

*"The things I had to do. I'm not proud of them, but I did them so you and your mother could have whatever you wanted."*

*"But all I wanted was you, Dad. Just to talk to, hang around with, be a friend."*

*"I know, but your mother wanted more."*

*"She still does," Emil said sadly.*

*"What about you?" Francis asked. "What do you want?"*

*Emil's eyes lit with a cold fire.*

*"Revenge."*

*"Better be careful," Francis said. "The Big Guy won't like that."*

*"You mean Frank Carson?"*

*Francis chuckled. "No, a bit bigger than him."*

*"But ..."*

*"Revenge is a dangerous animal," Francis said, tossing the ball to Emil. "Once you turn it loose, it can turn on you, even consume you."*

*"But it wasn't fair for him to take you away."*

*"I know, but fairness is never guaranteed."*

"What about justice?" Emil said, throwing the ball back.

"Whose justice?" Francis said without a hint of anger. "Who decides what is just?"

Emil didn't have an answer.

"It's time for you to go, son."

"No," Emil pleaded. "Why can't I stay?"

"It's not your time yet," Francis said, smiling.

"Will I see you again?" Emil asked.

"I don't know, son. If you let your rage control you, this may be the last time we meet."

"No!" Emil cried out.

The ball appeared as if out of nowhere. Emil caught it and looked for his father to toss it to, but the fog thickened, and his dad was gone.

He looked down at the ball, as a tear splashed on it.

He opened his eyes only to see the ceiling of a hospital room and a nurse changing his IV.

"What day is it?" Emil rasped.

It scared the nurse so bad she ran out of the room.

# THIRTEEN

Emil marched down the long road to recovery. Even after he was released from the hospital, he rehabbed every day, even after it wasn't needed. He started a weightlifting program coupled with a nutrition program designed to build strength. He worked out seven days a week, gaining muscle day by day. He gained thirty pounds of pure muscle during his time off. His first day back at the prison, Warden Tanzey called him into his office.

"Come in, Mr. Sorn. Have a seat."

"Thank you, sir."

"How are you feeling? You look really good."

"I feel fine, sir. Thank you for visiting me in the hospital."

"How did you know?"

"I could hear things happening even when I was in my coma."

"I didn't know that could happen."

"It can, sir, and she's wrong."

"Who's wrong?"

"My mother. It's not your fault that I got hurt."

"I appreciate that," Tanzey said. "I'd also appreciate hearing how this happened."

Emil gathered his thoughts.

"Inmate Carson intrigued me with his story of my father, but I knew something was wrong. He was giving me the story I've wanted for years and asking nothing in return. I interrupted him, and when I went back a couple of days later, I went prepared."

Emil reached into his shirt pocket and pulled out what looked like a pen. "I recorded the incident on this, sir."

"That's a bit James Bond, isn't it?" Tanzey said, eyeing the pen.

"I don't question methods that work, sir."

Emil set the pen on the desk and pressed play. Ten minutes later, the recording ended with the sounds of Emil being beaten nearly to death and the officers tasing Carson to rescue Emil.

The warden sat back in his chair pondering the recording for several minutes.

"It definitely fills some holes in the story. But I don't think it will hold up in court."

"I understand, sir. As long as you know the real story, that's all that matters."

"I am concerned, though, that you began an investigation without informing anyone."

"I am sorry for that, sir, but with all due respect, I wasn't sure how deep the rabbit hole went."

Tanzey eyed Emil. "And what would you have done if I ended up being the rabbit?"

Emil shifted uncomfortably in his chair. "I had thought about that, sir, and I honestly don't know."

Tanzey smiled. "I'm not the rabbit."

Emil visibly relaxed. "I'm glad, sir."

"We still have a problem, though."

"Which is?"

"You assaulted Carson first."

"Yes, sir. I knew he was setting me up after the threat. I

knew someone would be coming after me."

"So, you chose to strike first," Tanzey said thoughtfully.

"As strange as it seems, I considered that to be my only chance of survival. Had I been stronger, it might have worked."

"Yes, you weren't very imposing, but you seemed to have bulked up a little."

"Tried to."

"Keep it up, however, I am going to have to take disciplinary action."

"For defending myself?"

"No, you can defend yourself, but it has to be done right."

"By letting him beat the hell out of me?"

"No, you already tried that. It didn't work out too well."

"No, sir, it didn't."

"You cannot be the aggressor," Tanzey said. "We have rules and laws governing our actions. If we sidestep them, choose to ignore them, then we are no better than the people imprisoned here."

"So, we have to obey the laws, but these criminals can do whatever they want?"

"I see where this conversation is going. Being in prison is their punishment."

"It's not enough."

"Granted, but you and I don't get to make that judgment."

"Why not? If the system fails, why doesn't justice fall to those it belongs to—the victims?"

Tanzey sat back and looked at Emil with an appraising eye.

"Son, I'm gonna give you some personal advice. Let go of your anger and hate. A place like this will destroy you."

Emil exhaled and visibly relaxed.

"You're right, sir. I just get tired of seeing people do

heinous things and then sit in a cushy cell like they're on vacation."

"No argument there, but we have to; that's our job."

"Thank you, sir. I'll try."

"Good. Now I have to give you your punishment."

"Oh, I forgot."

"Officer Sorn, for two months, you will work in the Restricted Housing Unit only."

"RHU?" Emil said slowly. "Where the man is housed who murdered my father and tried to murder me? I don't know if I'll be able to do that, sir."

"I'm ordering you to. Either do it or you're fired."

Emil straightened in his chair.

"Yes, sir. Is there anything else, sir?"

"No, you're dismissed."

Emil got up to leave.

"Sorn."

"Yes, sir?"

"Look past the punishment and see the opportunity."

"Yes. sir," Emil said. He left feeling confused.

~

*Look past the punishment and see the opportunity. What does that mean?* Emil was still pondering the warden's admonition as he drove to work the next day.

"Day one of my sixty-day sentence," he said as he entered the RHU.

He started his first round and was greeted at the third cell by calls of "Hey, hey, look who it is. My old sparring partner, Emil Sorn," from Frank Carson as he walked up to the cell door. Emil kept walking without saying a word.

"C'mon, Emil, you look like you buffed up a little. You ready for round two?"

Emil gritted his teeth and kept walking. He didn't look back, but he could hear Carson chuckle.

Every thirty minutes, Emil had to make a round of the cells. Every time he came near, Carson took advantage of the opportunity to torment him. Emil did get a small payback. When he served lunch trays, Carson looked at his and said, "There's not anything extra on my tray, is there?"

Emil just smiled and said, "Bon appétit," before walking away. *Let him think I spit in his tray, or worse,* Emil thought.

When he collected the trays, Carson's hadn't been touched.

"Weren't you hungry, Mr. Carson?" Emil asked with a smile.

"You know why I didn't eat," he seethed. "You did something to my food. I want a lieutenant in here right now!"

"Calm down, Mr. Carson. I didn't do anything to your tray ... today," Emil said, letting the last word linger as an unfulfilled threat.

After a week of Carson's verbal abuse, countered by Emil's mental retaliation, the game grew stale. Carson seemed to settle down, but Emil knew he was just trying a different tactic.

# FOURTEEN

Please don't!" Carson yelled, followed by the sound of a fist hitting a body.

Emil went running to Carson's cell, to find him alone and bloody. He looked at Emil and smiled. Then a look of mock horror came over his face.

"No, Officer Sorn, don't hit me anymore," he said and then punched himself in the jaw so hard it knocked a tooth out.

"I need all available officers to RHU, now!" Emil called into his radio.

Three officers and the sergeant came running. After Emil explained what was happening, the sergeant ordered Carson cuffed and taken to the infirmary.

Emil went along to make sure Carson didn't make any wild accusations. When they got there, Carson started screaming that Emil wanted to beat him to death. The nurse on duty made Emil wait outside the examining room.

He kicked a cabinet in anger, and several bottles of pills fell out of it. Emil started picking them up, when he happened to notice the label on one. "Frank Carson, hypertension, take three times daily." An idea struck Emil.

He opened the bottle, looked at the pills, and then looked at several others. He saw some that looked almost identical. He dumped out Carson's real medication and replaced them with the others. As an afterthought, he looked at the other label. It said, "salt tablets."

*That should make him good and sick,* Emil thought with a smile.

He put things back in order just as a bandaged, moaning Carson was brought out. Emil rolled his eyes at the performance.

The officers took Carson back to RHU, where he collapsed on his bed and moaned even louder. One of the officers looked from Carson to Emil, patted Emil on the shoulder and said, "Good luck."

On Emil's next round, Carson said, "Officer Sorn, could I trouble you for a drink of water? My injuries are so severe that I can't make it to my sink without pain."

Emil kept walking, once again hearing Carson chuckle behind him. Carson tried to press charges against Emil for assault, but they didn't stick. The Warden gave him another sixty days in RHU for false accusations against staff.

Back and forth they went, like two dogs fighting over a bone. But as time passed, Carson's interest in the game faded, until one day when Emil passed, the prisoner didn't bother to speak.

"What's the matter, Carson? Did you forget to take your asshole pills today?"

"Major headache," he replied. "I don't feel like playing today, Officer Sorn."

Against his better judgment, Emil asked, "Do you want me to call medical?"

Carson raised an eyebrow at the compassionate offer. "No thank you, officer. I think a little sleep will help."

The rest of the day, Emil didn't disturb Carson. Carson didn't move, didn't even eat. He just slept all day. When the next shift came on, Emil informed them of Carson's headache and told them to be careful in case he was trying something.

The next day, Carson was just as bad.

"Are you taking any pain meds?" Emil asked him.

"The nurse gave me some Tylenol last night, but that barely made a dent in the pain."

Emil pulled his radio off his belt.

"Medical, please come to RHU."

"En route."

Five minutes later, the nurse was examining Carson.

"His blood pressure is through the roof. I'm going to double his blood pressure meds until he stabilizes," she told Emil.

"Have you been eating a lot of salty food?" she asked Carson.

"Only whatever I get on my tray."

"You should already be on a low-sodium diet. I'll double check with the kitchen."

"Thank you, nurse," Carson said as she left.

"And thank you, officer Sorn. I know we've been at odds lately. You didn't have to call the nurse."

"You're welcome," Emil said.

Three days later, Frank Carson died of a massive heart attack.

The warden summoned Emil.

He was pacing back and forth, clearly agitated. When Sorn came in, Tanzey commanded, "Sit!"

"When I said, 'See the opportunity,' that meant you were supposed to learn to control your anger by facing the person who makes you the most angry—not kill him!" Tanzey screamed.

"Sir, I had nothing to do with that."

Tanzey glared at him.

"You're telling me it was just coincidence that the man

you hated most in the world happened to pass away while you were assigned to his unit?"

"It does look suspicious, doesn't it?" Emil said. "Who assigned me to that unit?"

Tanzey was fuming.

"You're playing a dangerous game, Officer Sorn."

"How old was inmate Carson?" Emil said.

"I think he was in his sixties," Tanzey said, not sure where this was going.

"His charges were murder, institutionalized rape, drug trafficking—triple life sentence, if I'm not mistaken."

"Your point?"

"My point is, sometimes old people die. And no one is going to shed a single tear, least of all me, about some over-the-hill piece of trash finally getting what was coming to him; but I had nothing to do with it."

Tanzey glared at Emil.

"Get out!" he yelled.

Emil started toward the door, then turned back and asked, "Since Carson isn't in RHU anymore, can I have my punishment reduced?"

"No! Get out!" Tanzey screamed, picking up the heaviest book he could find and launching it at Emil.

Emil ducked through the door before the book hit it, leaving a crack in the glass.

Tanzey closed his eyes and leaned back in his chair for a few minutes. He sighed, walked around the desk, picked up the book to put it back, and noticed the title as he did: *Ethics in Corrections*.

# FIFTEEN

Emi realized if he wasn't careful, Warden Tanzey could not only fire him, he could even wind up behind bars. But Emil was careful, crossing every 't,' dotting every 'i,' handing inmates with a firm hand by never crossing the line. No longer interested in personal revenge, Emil committed himself to the long game. He transformed himself into the model CO, earning the respect of his fellow officers and his superiors.

Within a year, Emil Sorn was a sergeant running the evening shift. Officers started transferring to his shift ... officers who shared Emil's core belief that inmates were too coddled and had too many rights. That they played too many games with the system and never received any real punishment for their crimes.

On Emil's shift, disrespect or disobedience in any form was dealt with swiftly, severely, and quietly.

~

When Alice Macgregor started as a corrections officer at Larsan, she got noticed right away. She reminded most people of a taller version of Marilyn Monroe with larger breasts. Her allure went deeper than the mere measurements though. Her eyes smoldered when she stared at you and the left side of her mouth would curve up ever so slightly. She seemed to have all the confidence in the world. Truth be told, she always hated her shoulders. She felt they were too wide and secretly compared them to a linebacker. Most men were less concerned with her shoulders than what was several inches lower. In a place where many people either trudged or strutted, she sauntered, as if she was gliding on a cloud and nothing in the world could bring her down.

Alice had only worked in Larsan a month, and already every available officer on her shift (and a few who were unavailable) had asked her out; but not Emil.

Alice knew the power her body had over men and when Emil didn't succumb, she took it as a personal challenge.

Emil found her very attractive, but he didn't like work relationships. He had seen too many fail. She made a concerted effort to get under his skin.

One day she would wear too much makeup, the next day too much perfume. She made sure she had the tightest uniform she could fit into, to show off her curves. Emil noticed all these tactics but did his best to ignore them. Emil almost sent her home for being out of uniform. The inmates noticed too, and they paid very close attention to her when she came on the cell block. Finally, Emil sat her down and had a talk with her.

"Officer Macgregor—" Emil started.

"Alice," she interrupted.

"What?"

"Call me Alice."

"Officer Macgregor, I have been very pleased with your performance as an officer so far."

"Why, thank you."

"However, we need to have a discussion about your appearance and hygiene."

Alice felt like she had been slapped in the face.

"Excuse me?" she said, narrowing her eyes.

"There are days when you wear too much makeup, days when you wear too much perfume, and your uniform is too small," he said flatly.

She shot him an icy stare.

"Have you had one of these little talks with any of your other officers?"

"No. I haven't had to."

"Then I believe this may fall under the heading of 'sexual harassment.' Perhaps I should call my lawyer."

Emil pounded the desk with his fist so hard that it rattled.

"Who do you think you're talking to?" Emil demanded. "This isn't some stupid little cheerleader camp. This is real life! Do you know what some of these people have done? Assault, murder ... *rape*. What do you think they'd do to you if they got you alone in their cell? I'm trying to protect you, *and* my officers who would have to risk their lives to go in and rescue your stupid ass, and you threaten me with sexual harassment? Get out of my office. Go home and rethink where you work, and who you work around. Dismissed."

The sheer force of his chastising threw her off balance. When he said "dismissed," she found herself on her feet, without knowing how she got there. She stormed out of his office slamming the door behind her. She marched out of the prison with her head high, determined to not allow the hot, angry tears to leak down her cheeks while her fellow officers stared in bewilderment. Once she was safely behind the wheel of her car, she pounded the dashboard in frustration, let out a primal scream and let the tears flow, creating streaks of mascara down her face.

That evening she sat on her couch, still fuming, binge-eating moose-tracks ice cream from the carton while watching the news. The anchor reported on a story where a woman had been severely beaten and raped. He said that the man who did it was caught and would be getting years of jail time.

They showed a picture of him. "Dustin Brennley," the caption said. He looked like he was in his late twenties. She saw a look of mayhem in his eyes. The spoon froze in her hand, halfway between the carton and her mouth. Her imagination kicked into overdrive. She could see it, as if it had already happened, and she was reliving a memory. She was laying on the concrete floor, her clothes ripped, her body exposed, Dustin Brennley's face leering over her, his hand clawing at her ... "

Alice mentally shook herself. The thought sent chills down her spine.

*I hope we don't get him in Larsan,* she thought. Then she remembered what Emil had told her earlier. The thought hit her like a freight train. *There are hundreds of Dustin Brennleys already in Larsan, and I've been strutting around in front of them like a Playboy bunny in heat.*

She shuddered. and considered quitting but still couldn't get one man out of her mind, the man she was attracted to and who infuriated her at the same time. She decided to sleep on it.

In the morning things were clearer. She knew what she wanted to do and got ready for work early. When Emil started shift briefing, he always looked at each officer. Today, he stopped at Alice. She had on a uniform that was not skintight and very little makeup. He couldn't smell a cloud of perfume coming from her. He gave her just the slightest of nods as acknowledgment, which she returned.

One day, after a cell extraction that didn't go according to plan, Alice was sporting a fat lip, and Emil had a black eye and a broken nose. Medical checked them around shift change, and then Emil looked at Alice.

"Let's go get a drink. I'll buy."

She took the ice pack off her swollen lip and said, "You're kidding, right?"

He smiled. "Don't worry, the place has seats in the back with subdued lighting."

"OK, just one question."

"All right."

"Do you still think my ass is stupid?"

Emil chuckled.

"No, I think your ass is brilliant," he said, blushing just slightly.

She laughed, and they went on their first date. They had such a good time they agreed to a second, and then a third, and a fourth.

Three months later they stood in front of a justice of the peace and exchanged vows.

They bought a mortgage with a little blue house attached to it. It had a white picket fence and a quarter acre of lawn to mow. It was on the outskirts of Frost Creek, a little town about twenty miles away from the prison.

They started their lives together and were incredibly happy ... for a time.

# SIXTEEN

At work Emil and Alice stayed strictly professional. No flirting, no nicknames, nothing personal. At times, it seemed as though they didn't even like each other.

Nothing could be farther from the truth. Working around each other without the outlet of even a kind look or loving touch created an overwhelming sexual tension between them. Not being able to touch each other or acknowledge their love was more than they could take. It exploded as soon as they got home. It was rare for them to be dressed for longer than five minutes from the time they hit the front door, and usually they emerged from the bedroom hours later in search of food before returning to the bedroom.

Things were perfect, or so they seemed. They rarely talked about work or any serious issues, but when they did, their opinions and values were so far apart the discussion almost always ended in a fight, which, of course, would be settled in the bedroom.

Things were perfect in the bedroom, but the living room was a different matter. Outside of sex, they had little in common. She liked chick flicks and sitcoms; he preferred cop shows and prison drama. She listened to country music; he banged his head to heavy metal. She loved a romantic candlelight dinner on fine china; he would eat a burger every day. Her favorite line from a movie was, "I'll have what she's having," from *When Harry Met Sally*. His favorite scene was watching Boggs get dragged into a cell in *The Shawshank Redemption*. And serious discussion ended in a fight, and their fights inevitably ended up in the bedroom.

They say opposites attract. What they don't question is once they're together, is the bond as strong as concrete, or as weak as a cheap magnet?

~

Meanwhile, back at Larsan Prison, Arnold Falan sat peacefully on his bunk; a little too peaceful for an inmate doing fifteen years. His hands were folded on his lap, his back was straight and he was staring at his cell wall. He looked like a schoolboy who had just been chastised for bad posture. He sat and waited.

They swept in like a fast-moving storm. Four large men, all in full riot gear. The ERT's armor, gloves and helmets were all as black as night. Falan's cell door was popped open, and the team flooded in.

"Get down on the floor," they yelled.

Falan threw himself down on the cold concrete as they quickly cuffed him.

"Right leg secure!"

"Left leg secure!"

"Right arm secure!"

"Left arm secure!"

They called out their assignments with practiced precision.

Once secure, they ordered inmate Falan to face the wall while they searched his cell. They weren't gentle either. Books, papers, even the mattress went flying as they searched every nook and cranny. Finally, one of the team members approached Falan.

"Where is it?" Emil said as he raised the visor on his helmet.

"Ah, Sergeant Sorn," Falan cooed. "I wondered if that was you. How is your evening going?"

"Not too good, Falan. Now, where are the drugs?"

"Drugs?" Falan repeated as though he had never heard the word before. "What drugs?"

"You know exactly what drugs. You got your shipment in today."

Falan feigned confusion.

"I took a Tylenol today. Is that what you mean?"

Emil leaned down so that he was nose-to-nose with Falan, who was five inches shorter and fifty pounds lighter.

"Don't play with me, shithead!" Emil said.

"I'm terribly sorry that you didn't find what you were looking for, Sergeant," Falan lied.

"Collins, Lamants," Emil said.

"Yes, sir," the two officers answered.

"Take Mr. Falan to RHU."

"On what charge?" Falan protested.

Emil looked around the destroyed cell and said, "Failure to maintain cleanliness standards outlined in the inmate handbook."

"You can't ... " was all Falan got out before the two officers dragged him out of the cell.

Tompkins watched Emil closely.

"Are you really going to use that lame-ass charge?" he said.

"No," Emil said. "Find a better one. Something that will stick. I need him to stay in the hole for a while."

"You think his buyers will get nervous?"

"I hope so," Emil said. "Maybe if we shake a few trees something will break loose."

"He seemed like he knew we were coming," Tompkins said. "You think he was tipped off?"

"Absolutely, and I intend to find the tipper."

Two hours later, Emil came home looking like a dog that had been kicked all day.

"How did your sting go?" Alice said, leaning against the bedroom doorframe in a skimpy teddy.

"It didn't," he said, collapsing onto the couch.

"What happened?"

"Nothing. That's the problem. Six months of investigation led to nothing."

"How can that be?"

"It's like he knew we were coming."

She sauntered up to him and sat on his lap.

"Come on, baby, let it go. Things will work out," she said, kissing him.

He stared into space, barely realizing she was there.

"Six months ... " he said.

"You'll nail him eventually," she said, pulling off her teddy. "In the meantime, why don't you nail me?"

As if waking from a dream, Emil's eyes raked over his wife's stunning, naked body. His mouth went dry and the events of the day melted from his mind. His mouth met hers and she pulled him to her. She stood, breathless, grabbed him by the belt buckle and pulled him into the bedroom."

Emil couldn't sleep that night. Around three in the morning, he came out to the living room and watched some TV. About an hour later, Alice woke up and came out to the living room.

"What's wrong, baby?" she said while snuggling up beside him on the couch.

"I can't figure out who knew we were coming."

"Is that still bothering you?"

"There was the warden, the lieutenants, and my team."

"Why is it so important?"

"I need to know how that piece of trash got his drugs."

"Why is he a piece of trash?" she said.

He looked at her with mild surprise.

"Because he's an inmate."

"What are his charges?"

"I don't know."

"Then how can you make a judgment about him?"

"Because they're all scum."

"Some are, yes. But some are just people who made a mistake and got caught."

"I don't see it that way. Once an inmate, always an inmate."

"So, if someone gets out of jail and never commits another crime, they're still a scumbag inmate to you?"

"Yes."

Alice looked at Emil in a whole new light.

"There's something I've been meaning to tell you, but the time wasn't right. I believe now is the time," Alice said. "You remember meeting my sister, right?"

"Yes."

"What did you think of her?"

"Very pretty, like you, nice girl, smart, very polite."

"She did a year and a half for possession of drugs. Now what do you think of her?"

"I guess appearances can be deceiving."

"So, you now consider her to be a scumbag inmate?"

Emil didn't answer.

"You don't even want the rest of the story?" Alice said, her eyes burning with frozen fire. "You don't care that it was when she was just out of high school and got caught doing something stupid. You don't want to know that she's been clean for nearly ten years? His honor Judge Sorn has handed down a proclamation of guilt, and that is his final judgment on the subject."

"So, I'm not allowed to have an opinion anymore?" Emil said. "The man is the head of the household, but the woman is the neck and can turn him whichever way she wants, is that it?"

"No one can change your mind once it's made up. I was just hoping your mind wasn't made up on this."

"It is."

"Fine," she said, and then she got up and started toward the bedroom.

"There's just one question I want you to ask yourself," she said. "Would I be calling this inmate a 'drug-dealing piece of trash' if his name was Francis Sorn?"

# SEVENTEEN

Emil thought about what Alice had said for a long time. His prevailing thought always started with, *How dare she?* The next few days were tense. Emil worked lots of overtime trying to track down the insider to the drug ring. At least that's what Emil told himself, and it was half true. The other half of the truth was, Emil was avoiding his wife. Since their blowup, he had no desire to see Alice, much less talk to her.

As the investigation kept hitting dead ends, Emil's frustration grew. Not having his loving partner to comfort him magnified it. Alice felt it too. The house was uncomfortable when Emil wasn't there and even more uncomfortable when he was. Work was exactly the same. They were both professional. Finally, she couldn't take it anymore. She went to a bar to wash down her loneliness with alcohol.

She sat quietly in the back ignoring the many drinks that were sent her way by admiring drunks. She was so focused on her drink that she didn't even look up when she heard someone clearing his throat.

"Not interested," she said without looking.

"Officer Macgregor?"

"Officer Macgregor-Sorn," she corrected, identifying her new suitor. "Warden Tanzey?"

"Yes," he said. "May I sit down?"

"Of course," she said. "Is there something wrong at the prison?"

"No, no, I just saw you over here in the corner and thought I would rescue you from an army of admirers vying for your attention."

"And you would have no personal stake in this whatsoever," she said, eyeing his empty ring finger.

"You do me a grave injustice, ma'am," he said feigning wounded pride. "You are a married woman. Married to one of the brightest officers Larsan Prison has ever seen."

"Yeah," she said, with a far-off look. "He's the best."

"I sense I have offended," he said.

"No, if anything you proved the point that I have been trying to avoid for a while now."

"What point is that?"

"That Emil has two wives. And unfortunately, I'm not his first," she sighed.

Tanzey stared at his drink as though the answer would magically appear.

"Um?"

"That's right. There's nothing to say."

They just sat quietly for a few moments.

"Well, I should probably get home. I'm sure Emil will have a lot of paperwork on my desk in the morning."

"I'm sure he will," she growled.

Tanzey rose and bid her farewell, then stopped. "This career that you both have chosen is a difficult one, especially on relationships," he said. "Believe me. I know more about my lawyer than I do about my third wife."

Alice couldn't help but smile, "Thanks. I'll keep that in mind."

Looking around at the room full of leering eyes, she decided it was time to go.

On the way home, Alice did some soul-searching. By the time she got there, she had made up her mind. She wanted to make her marriage work, even if she had to fight for it.

An hour later, Emil slammed the front door closed, threw his coat across the room, and punched a hole in the wall. His rage inhabited his scream like a living thing, magnifying it.

Alice ran from the bedroom, already naked, in anticipation of Emil's arrival.

"What's wrong? Are you OK?" she asked.

"No, I'm not OK. I'm pissed."

"Why? What happened?"

"They let him out."

"Who?"

"Falan! After working for six months to catch him dealing, they let him out of RHU without even hearing the case."

"How can they do that?"

"Because he's a lieutenant's snitch. Suddenly evidence got 'misplaced,' and the lieutenant said there was nothing to charge him with."

Emil collapsed onto the couch. Alice sauntered over to him and started unbuttoning his shirt.

"C'mon, baby, leave work at work. I have something to take your mind off of it," she said as she rubbed her bare breasts against his exposed chest. Emil was so deep in thought he didn't even notice.

"I need to find a way to expose that lieutenant," he pondered. "Mm-hmm," she said, as she started kissing his neck and unbuttoning his pants. She pulled them off and started kissing him all up and down his body, rubbing her naked body against his.

Emil suddenly became aware of what she was doing, as

though he had just awakened from a dream.

"I'm not in the mood right now."

"C'mon, baby, I'll put you in the mood," she said, as she continued to kiss him, rubbing her firm, full breasts against his hardened chest.

"I don't want to be put in the mood. I need to think."

"Think about this," she said, as she climbed on top of him.

"Enough." he shouted. "I told you no!"

"Why, because you're pissed at some inmate and can't let it go?"

"You don't understand."

"You're right, I don't understand. Do you really hate them more than you love me?" she said, starting to kiss him again.

"Of course not."

"Then forget about them and screw me," she said, mounting him.

"I said no!" he said, throwing her off him.

She landed with a heavy thud, missing going right through the glass and wrought iron coffee table by mere inches. Pain shot through her body. She tried to breathe, but the impact had knocked the wind out of her.

Emil stood and approached her, but not to apologize, not even to help her up. He hovered over her, fists clenched, body taut, as if ready to beat down the heavyweight champion.

"No means no! You need to learn that just like those damn inmates!"

She lay there unable to move, barely able to breathe, feeling more helpless than she had ever felt.

His face was a mask of rage, his head beet-red, looking like he was seconds from exploding.

He took a step toward her when suddenly the phone rang. The sound jarred him to the reality of what he was about to do. He stopped, looked at the woman he loved cowering on the floor afraid of him.

He reached out his hand to help her up, but she recoiled. He pulled his hand back, and instead of helping her, he answered the phone.

"Yes. OK. I'll be right there."

"They need me at work," he told her.

She didn't respond, just stared at him.

He tried to say something else, but no words would come. Instead, he turned, dressed and left.

The cold floor gave her chills. If not for that, she might have stayed there all night. Physical and mental pain played tug of war with her.

Sobs wracked her body. Betrayal, guilt and horror filled her mind. Slowly, unsteadily, she got up, stumbled to the bedroom, and eventually fell into a restless sleep.

Hours later, he returned, found her in bed, and crawled in beside her. Neither one spoke. There were no words to say.

# EIGHTEEN

Some things are difficult to think and impossible to say. Unfortunately for Emil, one of those things is "I'm sorry." Two little words that might have saved his marriage.

Alice and Emil made a halfhearted attempt at counseling, but Emil just couldn't overcome that one obstacle. Within a month, he had moved out of their house and into an apartment in Larsan, just a mile away from the prison.

Her divorce lawyer said the settlement for the house would be fair; they would split it fifty-fifty. Emil thought he heard a slight chuckle before the lawyer hung up. Once Emil got the paperwork, he understood.

The deal was fifty-fifty all right—she got the house and he got the mortgage. Emil called Alice.

"Hello?"

"Yeah, I remember this tune. 'She got the gold mine, and I got the shaft.' No deal, baby!"

"Emil? What are you talking about?"

"I just read the lawyer's proposal."

"Oh."

"Yeah, 'oh.' I thought this was gonna be a no-fault divorce."

"My lawyer convinced me that I deserved more."

"So, the shyster lawyer that you're probably banging convinced you to steal every penny I've got? Guess what, sweetheart. I don't make that much. You remember; you used to do the bills."

"Yes, and there was always some unaccounted money. And for the record, even though it's none of your business, I'm not 'banging' anybody."

"That 'unaccounted money' is none of your business."

"What, are you taking after your daddy and running your own little side business in prison?"

Emil's silence was all she needed. She knew she had stepped over the line and hit him in the most vulnerable spot.

"Emil, I'm sorry. I didn't mean to ... "

"Yes, you did!"

*Click.*

And that was it; the fairy-tale marriage was over. It didn't end with trumpets blaring as they rode off into the sunset. It didn't even end with a bang, unless you count the phone being slammed down.

Neither of them let it disturb their work. They acted just the same as before ... strictly professional. And life went on.

~

"Sergeant Sorn, you have a phone call," an officer called over the radio.

"Hello?"

"Emil Sorn?"

"Yes?"

"This is Doctor Lewis at Memorial Hospital. Your mother was admitted this morning, and I ran some tests on her. I think you should come down to my office to discuss the results."

"What's wrong with her, doc?"

"I think it would be better to discuss this in person."

"Just tell me."

"All right. She has primary pulmonary hypertension."

"What does that mean?"

"In short, it means that her heart is failing."

"Can't you do anything about it? Medicine? Surgery?"

"The disease is far too advanced for any treatment to be successful."

"So, she's in a hospital bed waiting to die?"

"She is being treated as best we can, but at this advanced stage of the disease, there is not much we can do."

"Why didn't you find this sooner?"

"Quite simple. I checked her medical record and she hasn't been to a doctor in over fifteen years."

"She hates doctors."

"Be that as it may, you're her son. Did you notice any symptoms?"

"Like what?"

"Tiredness, fatigue, fainting spells ... "

"She did have some of those, but she would just say it's nothing. We haven't been on the best of terms, so she wouldn't tell me everything."

"Had treatment started when the symptoms first appeared, she would not be in this circumstance now."

"What are you saying, doc?"

"If you had been able to persuade her to see a doctor, she could've been treated and possibly gotten better."

"So, you're blaming me?"

"No, not at all."

"Yes, you are. You just said it—if I had been able to get her to see a doctor, she might've gotten better."

"Um ... I suppose I did say that."

"Yes, you did, you self-righteous son of a bitch! It's a good thing I didn't come to your office or I'd have you by the throat right now!"

"N-now there's n-no reason to get upset, Mr. Sorn," the doctor stammered.

"Oh, I think there's plenty of reason to get upset. What did you say your name was again? Lewis? Maybe I'll pay you a personal visit after I've gone to see my mother, who, according to you, I killed!"

The phone line went dead.

"Yeah, that's what I thought. Another self-important coward."

Emil hated hospitals ever since he'd been in one. The worst part for him was the smell; like antiseptic mixed with death. He paused outside room 320. He wasn't sure what he would face on the other side.

He grabbed the handle and went inside. His mom was sleeping in a bed with tubes and wires running from her to various machines. The sounds of monitors reminded him of several years ago, when he laid in a bed like this. It wasn't a pleasant memory.

She woke when he entered the room. She squinted trying to see who it was without her glasses.

When she focused on his face, she said, "Oh, it's you," obviously disappointed.

He walked up beside her bed.

"It's nice to see you too," he said, looking around at the machines that were keeping his mother alive.

"So, this is what it was like for you when I was in the hospital?"

She ignored him. He leaned closer to her.

"Maybe I should give you a good, hard slap across the face for not going to the doctor."

She cringed, knowing that he just might do it.

"You knew about that?"

"Of course I knew. I heard everything while I was in that coma."

"Everything?"

He smiled. "Everything."

"Why are you here?"

"Isn't it obvious? I'm a loving son come to see his poor, stricken mother, who's standing at death's door. But did my loving mother call me to say she's in the hospital? No. I had to find out from some schmuck doctor. Thanks, Mom."

The numbers on the machine that monitored her blood pressure started beeping faster.

"So now that I'm dying, you actually care?"

"Apparently. I'm here, right?"

"Just showing up doesn't count."

"Sure it does. If you had shown up at the doctor once in a while, neither of us would be in this room right now."

"I hate doctors, you know that."

"I'm sure the feeling is mutual," he muttered.

"What was that supposed to mean?"

"It means that if you had gone, the doctors could've taken care of you."

She stared into his eyes.

"That's what I had a son for."

"You're right, Mom. It's all my fault. My fault you're sick; my fault my marriage failed; my fault Dad was murdered; my fault we lived in poverty for most of my childhood. Everything's my fault."

She lay silent.

"You really believe it, don't you?" Emil said in disbelief. "It must be great to blame all your problems on someone else. It frees you from any and all responsibility."

"Truth is truth, painful or not," she said.

"You know," he mumbled "I came here to tell you I love you, but right now I don't even like you."

"You're just like your father, and you'll end up like him too," she said, hoping to win a point in the argument.

Instead, Emil grinned.

"That's the nicest thing you've said to me in years. Have a nice life," he said as he turned to leave. "Both hours of it."

Emil fumed on his way out. He needed to vent some rage. He looked for Dr. Lewis, but the doctor had left early, unexpectedly.

Rosemarie Sorn was buried three days later. It was a small ceremony for family and friends. About fifty people showed up.

As they were paying their respects to Emil, he noticed Alice walk in wearing a black dress that nicely complemented her figure.

*She looks just as beautiful as when I married her,* he thought.

He willed his feet to move, trying not to fall over them as he stared at the woman of his dreams.

"What are you doing here?" Emil asked her.

"It's good to see you too." She rolled her eyes.

"You know what I mean. I thought that you and she didn't get along."

"No, you're confusing me with you."

"She was the one who didn't even tell me she was in the hospital," he said, drawing stares as he raised his voice.

"I didn't come here for this," she said, turning to leave. "I came to pay my respects, but instead I'm leaving."

He grabbed her arm.

"I'm sorry. Please don't go," he pleaded.

Alice was stunned. "'I'm sorry'? 'Please'?" she repeated. "How did those words taste? I haven't heard them come out of your mouth in a long time."

"I just need someone to talk to. You wanna go get a drink?"

Emil braced himself for a refusal, but was pleasantly disappointed.

"OK, where to?"

Emil smiled. "I know just the place."

Twenty minutes later they were sitting at the same bar,

same booth where they'd had their first date.

"Nice," she said. "You bring all your dates here?"

"Yep, every girl I've dated in the last ten years I've brought here." He smiled and winked at her.

"Wow, that must be quite a list."

"I can count them on one finger." He noticed how great she smelled.

She smiled. "Look, I really am sorry about your mom," she said. She reached out to hold his hand across the table.

"I tried to talk to her. I went to see her in the hospital, and she just wasn't interested in reconciliation at all."

"She wasn't happy to see you?"

"About as happy as a whale is to see a harpoon. She wanted to blame me for everything. The doctor said she could've been treated if she had gone to see him, but she hadn't been to a doctor in fifteen years."

"I had no idea. But you know she loved you."

"The last words she said to me were 'You're just like your father, and you'll end up like him too.'"

"Oh."

"Not sounding like a lot of love there."

"What were your last words?"

"I don't remember," Emil lied.

"You don't remember your final words to your dying mother?"

"I think it was something like, 'Have a nice life.'"

"Not a lot of affection there either."

"I had already told her I loved her, and she spat in my face."

"You two never were what you'd call close."

"Ah reckon yer right there, little filly."

Alice laughed. "I miss your sense of humor. It's what I liked the most when we were together."

"I miss you," Emil said. "I didn't realize how much until now."

"Listen ... Emil ..."

"I'm sorry," he said earnestly. "I'm sorry for the mistakes I made when we were together. I'm sorry I hurt you. I'm sorry we divorced instead of working things out. I'd like another chance, if you're willing."

Alice sat silently. She studied Emil's face, looking for any sign of deception, but saw none. Her face reflected her conflicted emotions. Slowly, she spoke.

"I miss you too at times. When things were good, we were great together," she said with a far-off look. "But I'm seeing someone."

Emil's face fell so far he'd have had to go downstairs to pick it up. For her sake, though, he recovered and tried to look impassive, even though his heart was in a thousand pieces.

"So, is it serious?"

She fidgeted uncomfortably in her seat.

"Well, yes. He gave me a ring."

"You're not wearing it."

"I came to the funeral straight from work, and I never take the ring to work."

"Who is he? Where did you meet him? Do I know him?"

"OK, Dad," she said with a laugh. "I'll be home on time and won't scratch the car."

He smiled in spite of himself.

"Sorry, just curious."

She smiled back.

"Who he is, is none of your business. Where I met him is around town. Do you know him? No," she said while avoiding his eyes, bracing for the worst.

Emil swallowed hard, forcing his pride and anger down.

"Does he treat you good?"

"Wonderful. Like a queen."

"You deserve to be treated right. I'm happy for you. Really I am."

She looked at him and saw no sign of anger, only disappointment and resignation. Her heart went out to him.

"I have to go."

"I understand. I'll walk you out."

He held the door open for her as she got in her car.

"You really have changed."

She reached up and kissed him on the cheek, and then she drove away.

Emil slowly got into his car and drove.

# NINETEEN

Weeks passed. Emil felt like he was trapped in limbo. Still, he had a job to do, and he did it well.

That included his dealings with thug named Dustin Brennley. Triple homicide, multiple aggravated assaults, rape – Brennley was a problem child, no doubt about it. He created enough chaos in the prison to land him in RHU more times than he could count.

To call him Emil's least favorite inmate would be like calling the universe "kinda big." As far as Brennley was concerned, the feeling was mutual, and did everything he could to aggravate Emil.

When the report came to Emil that Brennley had thrown urine on an officer, Emil stormed straight to his cell to take him to RHU. When he refused to go, Emil was ready to spray him with pepper spray until Lieutenant Carey was called to the disturbance.

"What's going on here, Sergeant?"

"Inmate Brennley is going to RHU, sir."

"For what offense?"

"Throwing urine on an officer, sir."

Brennley saw his opportunity and took it.

"It's a lie!" he told the lieutenant.

"Sergeant Sorn is always trying to get me, sir. He watches me night and day. I live in fear of what he'll do next," Brennley said, while pretending to sob.

The lieutenant looked indignant. Emil was waiting for the order to spray the inmate, when the lieutenant turned on him.

"What do you have to say for yourself, Sergeant?"

"What do you mean, sir?"

"Defend yourself against these allegations."

Brennley stopped sobbing and peeked an eye out from between his hands.

"Right here, right now, sir?" Emil asked, not believing it.

"Yes."

Emil did his best to control his temper.

"My defense is that inmate Brennley is lying, and if you go ask the officer that he threw urine on, you will see. I further request inmate Brennley's medical records. If he has any communicable diseases, especially HIV, that he be charged with assault with a deadly weapon."

"Don't you think that's a little extreme, Sergeant?"

"No, sir. If my officer contracts AIDS, hepatitis, or anything else because of this incident, he won't think it's extreme either."

"You're blowing things out of proportion, Sergeant. Right now, I have two individuals who each say the other is lying. The only reasonable course of action is for both parties to drop the issue and pretend it never happened."

Emil felt numb. He became vaguely aware that he was still holding a can of pepper spray, but right now it was a toss-up between who he wanted to spray more, the inmate or the lieutenant.

"That can't be your decision, sir," Emil said.

"But it is, Sergeant Sorn. You, Mr. Brennley, will not mention this issue again. Is that understood?"

"Oh ... yes sir," Brennley said.

## CHAPTER 19

"And you, Sergeant Sorn ... you have come dangerously close to insubordination. I may have to report this."

Then he turned and strolled away. Emil was dumbstruck, and Brennley enjoyed every minute of it. Emil saw him grinning from ear to ear and had to walk away.

Brennley called after him.

"Hey, Sorn, tell your officer I know a good dry cleaner!"

Emil forced himself to keep walking, while Brennley howled with laughter.

~

Later that night the room was dark and the air was close. The steady, rhythmic breathing was punctuated by an occasional muffled sob.

She lay on her back, eyes closed, wishing she were unconscious. The pain and the stench that emanated from his body made her want to vomit. Unfortunately, her mouth was taped shut.

Her hands were tied behind her back, making it even more painful as he pressed his body against her over and over. Her shirt and bra had both been torn. Her pants and underwear were shoved down to her ankles, forming impromptu leg shackles.

She tried to resist and was rewarded with a black eye and a broken rib. He was bigger, stronger and faster than she, and he knew it. Once she realized she was outmatched, she tried to scream. That netted her three loose teeth and a hairline fracture in her jawbone.

She squeezed her eyes shut even tighter, trying to think of anything other than the heinous act that was being inflicted on her. Her thoughts wandered to the recent past.

*She was doing her last round on her shift. The block had been quiet today, eerily quiet. She shrugged it off, though.*

My shift is almost done, *she thought.* I'll let the next shift know to be extra careful.

*With twenty-eight minutes left in her shift, she was thinking about going home and curling up with a good book. Perhaps she would call that special someone and see if he wanted to come over and watch a movie.*

*"Excuse me, Officer Sorn," an inmate said, interrupting her thoughts.*

*"It's Officer Macgregor," she corrected.*

*"My apologies," he said. "So, the divorce is final then?"*

*"What can I do for you, Mr. Brennley?" she asked, ignoring his question.*

*"I'm having a problem with my bunk," he said. "One of the screws is loose, and I don't want to fall onto a concrete floor in the middle of the night."*

*"Understandable," she said. "Let me take a look."*

*As soon as she walked over to the bunk, the cell door slammed shut. A cold chill ran down her spine as she reached for her OC. He was too quick and knocked it out of her hand.*

*Knowing she was in trouble, she aimed a vicious kick at his groin. He deftly ducked it and turned out her lights with a massive right to the jaw. She crumbled to the floor, as the world swooned around her.*

Her thoughts snapped back to the present. Something was different. He was slowing down. He was almost done. Unimaginable horrors paraded through her mind, each one worse than the one before. She was pulled back to harsh reality by the sound of the cell door crashing open and electricity crackling through the air.

Her groin felt like it was on fire, as she tried to scream in pain. Her mind had enough and mercifully faded to black.

# TWENTY

Alice woke to a different kind of rhythm. The steady beeping of machines told her she was still alive and in a hospital. The pain emanating from several places on her body had been dulled with medication. Her mind also seemed somewhat numb.

*Must be a sedative.*

She tried to straighten up, causing the pain to reawaken. She stopped moving and it subsided. With nothing better to do, she started chastising herself.

*How could I have been so stupid? Why didn't I just call maintenance?*

The answer came to her straightaway.

*Because you weren't paying attention. You were thinking about where you wanted to be instead of where you were.*

She faded back to sleep remembering the news report she had watched so long ago.

~

The next day, Emil came on shift and was briefed by the sergeant on duty.

"We had a quiet night, until Brennley got a hold of an officer. Beat her pretty badly, and raped her."

"I assume the S.O.B is in RHU."

"Oh yeah. We had to spray and taze him."

"How's the officer?" Sorn replied

"I don't know. She was taken to Memorial hospital, I haven't had time to call and check on her."

"Who was it?"

"Officer Macgregor."

Emil froze. "Alice Macgregor?"

"Honestly I don't know many officers by their first names. I haven't been on this shift very long. There's a lot of names to learn. Thank God for nametags, right?" he chuckled.

Emil did his best to maintain his composure through the rest of the briefing. He then briefed his shift, and started his rounds. His thoughts walked a tightrope between hatred and revenge toward Brennley, and concern for Alice. The divorce had not been pleasant, but there were times when he truly missed her. He had even asked her out again. Being around her just made him feel better, perhaps even made him a better man.

Emil passed an office door and chills suddenly ran down his spine, remembering the previous day, he backed up, stared at the door labeled 'Lt. Carey.' Emil could feel his rage rise like bile in the back of his throat before exploding through the closed door, destroying the lock, and shattering the glass.

"You!" he screamed. "You made this happen!"

"Excuse me, *sergeant*?" Carey said, with a purposeful emphasis on the last word. "Watch your tone, or this prison won't be your concern anymore!"

"You ball-less piece of crap! You are to blame for my officer being attacked," Emil exploded. "Your little stunt the other day empowered Brennley."

"I fail to see what inmate Brennley has to do with anything."

"If you had let me do my job, he would've already been in RHU, and none of this would've happened. This is your fault. If she dies, I will personally make sure you are charged as an accomplice to homicide."

Lt. Carey rose, a seething volcano about to erupt, but still not quite tall enough to stare Emil directly in the eye.

"Take a good look around," Lt. Carey said with stony resolve. "You won't be here after Tanzey read my report. Dismissed."

Emil refused to move for a long moment while he considered tearing his superior limb from limb. A dangerous smile tweaked the corners of his mouth. He could see Carey shaking is fear.

"Coward," Emil spat on the floor at Carey's feet, then gave him a crisp salute, did a regulation about face and marched out of the office, leaving the shattered door sagging on its hinges behind him.

He quick-stepped to the changing room, and put three fist-sized dents in his locker. After his adrenaline crashed, he went to the infirmary to have his hand examined. Only one bone was broken.

The following day, Warden Tanzey called Emil into his office.

"Mr. Sorn, have a seat," The warden commanded. "I read Lt. Carey's report. Do you have anything to add?"

"Only my opinion, sir."

"Let's hear it."

Emil decided to make his true feelings known. *You can say anything you want on your last day at work, right?* he allowed a wry grin to cross his mind, although it didn't reach his face.

"Lt. Carey is not suited to be in any position of authority in a prison setting."

"Interesting, go on."

"He lacks the courage and intelligence to do the job, he

is a liability and a threat to the security of this prison and the officers working under him. He is also directly responsible for the attack on an officer by inmate Brennley."

"That is a very serious charge, sergeant. Do you have any proof?"

Emil shifted in his seat. "Just documentation sir, mostly my reports."

"Yes, I've read them," Tanzey said. "I just have one question; how did you manage to keep from putting a fist-sized dent in Carey's forehead, instead of your locker?"

The grin now reached Emil's face. "It wasn't easy sir."

Tanzey leaned forward, "And yet, you did. Every time you're faced with a challenge, something someone else doesn't want to deal with, you manage to do it. You take care of business, no matter what."

"Yes, sir. Thank you, sir."

"So, you expect me to discipline a member of my staff, merely on your word?"

"Not my work alone, sir. If you talk to other officers, I'm sure they would say the same things."

Tanzey leaned back in his chair and appraised the sergeant for a moment.

"Do you trust me, Mr. Sorn?"

"Of course, sir."

"I know your record. I know you hate injustice with a passion, that you'll do all that you can to prevent it, or destroy it."

"I've never heard it put quite that way sir, but I suppose that's an accurate description."

"I will take care of Lt. Carey."

"Thank you, sir." Emil started to rise.

"Hold on. It comes at a price."

Emil eyed the warden sideways, like a mouse appraising a hawk.

"What price, sir," he said as he settled back into the chair.

"I have an inmate that needs to be ... *handled*."

"What, exactly, do you mean, *handled*?"

"You know exactly what I mean."

The enormity of what was being asked weighed down on Sorn like a steamroller with an elephant driving it.

"No."

"No, you don't understand, or no, you won't do it?"

"No, I won't do it."

"I could write you up for insubordination."

"You're going to write me up for not accepting a hit on an inmate? Good luck with that one ... sir."

Tanzey pursed his lips and tried a different tact. "Seargeant Sorn. Emil. This is ... personal."

"Personal for who?"

"It's personal!" Tanzey repeated.

"I'll tell you what's personal for me. Jail time., I don't want to do any," Emil retorted.

"That won't happen. I'll cover for you."

"Do you know how many times I've heard that line before? Emil laughed. "Why do you think half the lieutenants have less seniority than me, and I'm still a sergeant?"

"Ok, how about a promotion? God knows you deserve one."

"No."

"To captain?"

"N... What?" Sorn thought about it. "Sorry, that still only lasts until I get arrested. Not interested."

"You could still get arrested."

"For what?"

"Well, it seems to me that you don't have a problem with killing inmates." Tanzey said, the threat hanging like the proverbial Sword of Damacles over Emil's head.

"No comment Mr. Sorn? Perhaps a small reminder. Inmate Morilli—you shot him in the chest point blank on your first day. And then there's the mysterious demise of inmate Carson, the man accused of murdering your father. Neither of these incidents was thoroughly investigated."

Tanzey leveled a stare at Emil.

"Perhaps a closer look into these incidents is warranted. What do you think, Mr. Sorn?"

"I think you're blackmailing me to do your dirty work." Emil struggled to control his temper. "I still won't do it."

Tanzey stood and fumbled with a paperweight on his desk, a gaudy bauble given to him by his first wife when he first made warden. He wasn't sure why he kept it.

"I appreciate your integrity Mr. Sorn. You are free to go."

Emil nodded, started by the change in Tanzey's demeanor. He stood, turned and reached for the door.

"Don't you want to know who?" Tanzey asked

Emil froze. Through clinched teeth he said, "No!"

"Brennley."

Emil's hand froze on the doorknob. "Dustin Brennley?" he breathed.

"Yes."

"Call me, Captain Sorn," he said as he turned the knob and walked out the door.

~

Emil called the hospital to check on Alice. A nurse in ICU talked to him.

"She's stable and resting."

"When can I come see her?"

"She shouldn't have visitors for a day or so. She needs to regain some strength."

"Thank you. What room is she in?"

"Four-fourteen."

He hung up the phone and called a friend who worked at a Larsan Alliance Chemicals.

"Chuck, I need a favor."

Later that evening Emil sat in his backyard, at his picnic table. He had an open pack of Camel cigarettes, just like the ones the inmates bought from commissary.

The pack only had three cigarettes left in it. He took one out with his gloved hand and dipped the tip in an open bottle with the letters NaCN on it. Then he put the cigarette back in the pack and sealed it in a plastic bag.

He quickly put the lid back on the bottle and returned it to the lab he had borrowed it from, with the cover story that he wouldn't have to worry about those pesky coyotes anymore.

The next day Emil's officers descended on inmate Tyler's cell like a fast-moving storm. Before he knew what had happened, his cell was being torn apart.

The officers didn't find much, but it was enough to put him in RHU. Sergeant Sorn personally supervised the search. They put Tyler in his RHU cell and left.

On his way out, the sergeant paused, reached into his pocket, and pulled out an open pack of cigarettes. He tossed them to the RHU officer.

"Here, we found these in his cell. Get rid of them."

"Yes, sir."

Emil turned and walked away with a smug look on his face, but doubt tugged at the edges of his mind. He went to Central under the pretense of checking up on things, but his eyes were glued to the RHU camera.

It took the RHU officer nearly forty minutes to start his rounds. Emil watched impatiently as he finally took the cigarettes to cell six—Brennley's cell. Emil watched with satisfaction as Brennley took the pack.

His happiness quickly turned to horror as he watched Brennley offer the officer a cigarette, and he took it. Emil was transfixed as he watched the scene play out on a small, black-and-white monitor. He couldn't get there in time to take it from the officer, and to even try would reveal his plan. He was stuck. All he could do was hope that the odds were in his favor.

The officer had a one-in-three chance of survival. Both inmate and officer smoked their cigarettes nonchalantly, having no idea of the danger they were in.

Thirty seconds had gone by, and neither man had tumbled to the floor. Emil now worried about the other thing that could happen, which is absolutely nothing. There was no guarantee that his plan would even work.

Two minutes had passed. The officer moved on to do the rest of his rounds, and Brennley finished his cigarette and went to bed.

*Nothing!* Emil thought bitterly.

"Are you all right, sir?" the control officer asked, startling Emil.

"Yes, I'm fine. I want that officer written up for handing in contraband."

"Yes, sir."

Emil went about his normal business but checked back in on RHU twice. Nothing had happened. Brennley was sleeping peacefully, and the officer seemed fine.

Emil chewed him out for handing in the cigarettes, even though that was part of his plan. It was a little payback for making him worry about the officer. Emil reluctantly went home at the end of his shift, but he couldn't sleep.

The next day, he resisted the urge to go in early and showed up right on time. He found out that the RHU officer from last night had called in sick. He first thought was that the officer had gotten the wrong cigarette and it had just made him sick. But then he checked Brennley, and he was sick too.

Things just weren't making sense. Two more days went

by. The officer came back to work, and Brennley felt better. Emil thought he would have to try again, until ...

"Emergency in RHU! Medical personnel needed immediately!"

Emil ran to RHU. When he got there, Brennley was in the middle of a convulsion, foaming at the mouth.

"We need to get him to the infirm now!" the nurse said.

Emil ordered three officers to escort him, just in case he was faking. They took him to medical, leaving only Emil and the RHU officer to search the cell.

Emil quickly found the empty pack of cigarettes, and the last one that was still lit. He pretended to sniff them, but was careful not to inhale.

"Nothing here," he said and quickly flushed both down the toilet.

The officer looked at him questioningly, but realizing that they were the cigarettes he had gotten chewed out for, quickly dropped his unasked question. They continued to search, when Emil produced a half empty can of almonds.

"What's this?"

"It's the same brand they order from commissary, but according to the date, it expired two years ago." Emil smelled them and recoiled. "They don't smell right. I'll take this to medical. Tell me if you find anything else."

By the time he got to medical, it was too late. Brennley was dead. The RHU officer filled out his official report, and then he made a separate report stating his personal opinion of the whole incident, which he kept at home for a rainy day.

~

"Covering cyanide with rotten almonds ... very nice," Warden Tanzey said, without much enthusiasm. "I'll stay long enough to make sure the official report sticks; then I'm done. I've had enough of this place."

Emil just nodded.

# TWENTY-ONE

Emil entered Alice's hospital room carrying a box of chocolates. He stopped and stared at the sleeping form that he barely recognized. Her face was bruised and bandaged. Her arm was in a cast, and there were myriad tubes and wires running to and from her body.

Rage began to build within Emil, but he realized that it was useless. He had already taken his revenge on the man who had done this. He slowed his breathing and let the rage bleed away.

Her eyes fluttered open. She turned toward Emil and managed a weak smile, swallowed and tried to speak. At first it was only a rasp, but after a few tries she was able to croak out, "What are you doing here?"

Emil returned the smile.

"Are you kidding? I bring every injured officer chocolates."

She laughed, which made pain shoot through her body, causing her to cringe.

Emil reached for her.

"I'm sorry. I didn't mean to hurt you."

The pain began to subside, and her smile returned.

"I know you didn't," she said, with a deeper meaning reflecting in her eyes.

"You look great."

"I look worse than I did on our first date."

"You looked great to me. Still do."

He could see the torment in her eyes. He reached down and gently held her hand. Electricity shot through her at his touch. Tears welled up in her eyes, as her heart began to melt.

"Emil," she said softly. "Listen, I ... "

Just then the door opened, and in walked Warden Tanzey holding a bouquet of flowers.

Everyone in the room froze. The tension was thicker than the polar ice pack.

"What's going on?" Tanzey slowly asked.

"You're kidding me, right?" Emil said to Alice. "Is he ... "

"I've been seeing Gordon for about two months now," Alice confessed.

"Gordon?"

She sighed.

"Gordon Tanzey."

"You weren't satisfied with a sergeant. Had to go to the top, huh?" Emil spat.

"It's not like that," Alice protested through a wave of pain.

"You got a problem with me, Sorn?" Tanzey asked.

"No, it's just that you're so, you know ... old."

"You wanna say that again, Captain?" Tanzey asked through gritted teeth.

"Captain? When did that happen?" Alice interrupted, trying to change to subject.

"Yesterday!" Tanzey snorted. "But it might be the shortest promotion in history."

"Are you threatening me?" Emil asked. "Just remember who called who into their office asking for a favor. If I go down, I'm dragging you along for the ride."

"You wouldn't dare. You'd be implicating yourself," Tanzey said.

"What the hell are you two talking about?" Alic yelled, sending her into spasms of pain.

"I took care of the scumbag that attacked you," Emil said.

"You mean *we* took care of the scumbag," Tanzey said.

"I don't remember you lifting a finger or taking one ounce of risk. In fact, your only contribution was to make me captain."

"You've got to be kidding me. I'm the one who ordered you to do it, and you had ice cubes for feet. 'Oh, I don't want to do it, I'm afraid I might get caught and go to jail,'" Tanzey said, mocking Emil.

Emil clenched his fist and started toward Tanzey.

"Wait a minute." Alice said. "So, you're telling me that you"—pointing to Tanzey—"ordered him to kill an inmate, and you"—pointing to Emil—"carried out the hit on his orders?"

They looked at each other.

"That pretty much sums it up, yeah," Tanzey said.

She lay there staring at them. A thousand thoughts tumbled through her head. She seemed to go catatonic for a moment.

Tanzey and Emil stood there looking at her. They shuffled uncomfortably waiting for her to say something ... preferably, which one she would choose to spend the rest of her life with. She shook herself, as if waking from a nightmare.

"Get out," she whispered.

They looked at each other.

"Which one?" Emil asked.

"Both."

They were stunned.

Tanzey recovered first. "Honey, you don't mean that; you're just tired. You need to get some rest."

She looked up at him with fire in her eyes.

"Don't talk to me like a child! I mean exactly what I said. Get out, both of you. I never want to see either of you again."

"But why?" Emil asked. "Look what we've done for you."

"Really? OK, let's look at what you've done for me. Criminal conspiracy and murder? What, a get-well card wasn't enough? I just can't believe that either of you thought this is what I would want."

"But you don't have to be afraid of him anymore," Tanzey said.

"No, I have to be afraid of you two. You don't understand. I can never trust either of you again, and it's just too painful to see two good men, men I loved, reduced to acting like criminals. Consider this my resignation. I won't step foot back inside that prison."

Both men were stunned. This reaction had never entered their minds. They'd thought they would be the conquering heroes, but now they were crushed, defeated.

"What will you do now?" Emil asked, hoping to regain some small measure of acceptance.

"I don't know," she replied thoughtfully. "I've been dealing with broken people from the punishment side for so long. Maybe it's time I started dealing with them from a healing and prevention side."

Tanzey chuckled, in spite of himself.

"What're you gonna do, open a mission?"

The flame rekindled in Alice's eyes.

"That's exactly what I'm going to do. All you two think about is hurting people; it's time someone started helping them. Now get out, both of you."

"But—" Emil tried to say.

"Get out!" she threw the closest thing she could grab.

They both ducked as the telephone sailed over their heads and collided with the wall, leaving a gaping hole.

"Get out!" she screamed again, grabbing a book from her nightstand and throwing it at them.

"What the hell's going on here?" a large nurse bellowed as stormed into the room.

"We were just leaving." Tanzey said.

The two men turned and left the room. With nothing left to say, they trudged toward the elevator. Each of them felt as though their heart had been ripped out. They rode to the lobby together in silence, and then left the building without speaking to each other again.

True to his word, Warden Tanzey stayed long enough to conclude the investigation into Brennley's death, stating that he saw no reason to call it anything other than accidental.

The next day, he turned in his resignation and retired a broken man. What should have been the happiest time in his life had become the saddest.

True to her word, Alice never set foot inside the prison again and never spoke to either man again.

# TWENTY-TWO

**W**ithout a warden, Emil became the top-ranking official at the prison. But something had changed in him. Whatever tiny seed of happiness Alice planted in him died that day in the hospital.

Emil reacted the only way he knew how. He threw himself into his job, changing rules to favor officers instead of inmates, making penalties much harsher on inmates, and going about the business of regaining control of the prison.

The prison became his world, and he ruled it with an iron fist. Inmates tried to fight back in whatever way they could—physically, through lawsuits, even attempted hits on Emil himself. Nothing worked; one by one Emil's opposition fell, and his new order took over.

The prison began to settle down and became more than just a garbage dump where assaults and riots were common. Once inmates realized that the old ways of them running the prison were ending, they fell in line.

As the prison calmed, Emil grew more restless. He found that he missed getting into scrapes and thumping a few inmates now and then.

Although the inmates no longer posed a serious threat, Emil couldn't shake a foreboding sense of impending anxiety. It was as if he was waiting for someone to burst his bubble. The state assigned a new warden to Larsan; Alton Randall Bennington III. He was small in stature, a mouse of a man, a political appointee who had never set foot inside a prison, let alone run one.

*I've given my life to this prison,* Emil thought. *I'll be damned if I let some little pipsqueak prick take it away from me.*

Emil made a quick phone call, them took him to lunch before touring the prison and asked him all about his career and life. By the time they drove back to the prison, Emil had a plan in mind.

He took Bennington on tour of the loudest, worst, most unruly block of inmates that Larsan had. By the time the tour ended at the warden's office, Emil could tell Bennington was terrified. He didn't mention that he had told one of his sergeants to spread the rumor that the new warden was going to double the prices of the inmates' commissary.

Seizing the opportunity, Emil "confessed" that he didn't have much of a background in management and hated going to the many conferences and political rallies that the state wanted him to attend. Bennington's eyes lit up.

"I could take that burden away from you, Captain," he said.

"Really?" Emil said. "How so?"

"We could be a team. I could do the upper management chores and go to the conferences, and you could run the day-to-day operations."

"That's a great idea," Emil said. "I never would've thought of that."

And so the prison remained firmly in Emil's control.

~

Every year, Emil took a special trip to the Eternal Rest Cemetery, on the outskirts of Larsan.

## CHAPTER 22

"Hey, Dad," Emil said to the small marble stone, with the words "Francis Sorn" engraved on it. "How've you been?"

He paused to look around at the trees starting to blossom, while swallowing hard to force down the lump in his throat.

"I would've brought you some birthday cake, but I don't think the groundskeepers liked cleaning that up last year," he said. He paused to chuckle. "I see they put Mom right beside you. That must suck. First she nagged you to death, now she'll be nagging you throughout eternity. On a different note, I'm still divorced and still not happy about it. I still miss you. I wish you could've been there when I was growing up, but it didn't turn out that way."

Emil's eyes started to mist. "Well, I gotta go, Dad. I love you. You take care."

He sauntered over to an older, more run-down section of the cemetery. He looked through the rows until he came across a familiar sight. Emil walked up to the gravestone, which had a slight stain on one side, and the name "Carson" on the front.

"Hey, Frank, it's that time of year again," he said to the gravestone. "Well, no use mincing words; might as well get to it."

Emil glanced around to make sure no one was near and then unzipped his pants. A yellow stream soon flowed down the Carson name. When done, Emil zipped up and walked away.

"See ya next year, Frank."

# TWENTY-THREE

The idea started in a bar, and like most ideas so conceived, it should've stayed there.

Emil sat at the bar of his favorite watering hole, The Frosty Mug. He was nursing his third beer while watching the game when a news flash came on the TV.

Police had arrested a man accused of holding a family hostage, robbing them, and raping their fourteen-year-old daughter. Emil just shook his head.

*I'll have him in Larsan soon enough.*

"Now that's the problem with society today," a large, drunk man said from a few barstools down. "This piece of shit is gonna waste thousands of taxpayers' dollars—*my* dollars—defending himself, and then he'll get out in a few years and do it again."

The man was waving his shot glass at the TV angrily.

"You oughta have your nuts cut off!" he bellowed at the TV. "They should tie you down and let that girl you raped do it, so that you can't rape no more."

A thought began to stir in Emil's mind.

"Whadda you think, buddy?" the man slurred in Emil's direction.

"I think you may be right," he pondered.

He finished his beer, said good night to the man, and went to the prison.

"Workin' late tonight, Cap'n?" Sheira, the night receptionist, asked.

"Just need to check a few things," he answered.

She buzzed him in.

He walked through the entire prison looking for rooms that were seldom or never used. He was just about to give up when he came to room 114.

It was a large, indoor gymnasium that was used for inclement weather. He searched it thoroughly and considered the rest of his plan. Looking up, he saw a lone security camera.

"Maintenance, report to room one fourteen," he said into his radio.

"Yes, sir."

Within five minutes the maintenance man had arrived.

"Check that camera," Emil told him. "I think it's broken."

The maintenance man got a ladder and climbed up to check it.

"It seems to be working fine, sir."

"It's broken!" Emil said, with menace in his voice.

Crossing Captain Sorn was not something you wanted to do if you wanted to stay healthy and employed. The maintenance man looked at the camera and then at the captain, and he got the message. He unplugged the power wire and the video-feed wire.

"Sir, I'm afraid this camera's broken. It won't be fixed for ..."

"Indefinitely." Emil said, picking up the verbal cue.

"Yes, sir. The parts are on back order. I'm not sure when I'll get them in. Sorry about that, sir. You'll have to do without a camera in this room for a while."

"That's all right. You did your best," Emil said.

The maintenance man went back to the tool room, checked that he was alone, and then made a short notation in his personal notebook.

~

There is a fine line between hard-nosed and brutal, and Emil Sorn was about to cross it.

The next night, smoke filled the air as six bodies crowded around a small table. Each man looked at the other with an air of curiosity tinged with distrust.

"Show 'em." Emil said, chewing on a cigar.

"Pair of jacks."

"Three deuces."

"Two pair."

The other two had folded, leaving only Emil to reveal his hand. Pausing for dramatic effect, he slowly lay down a straight flush. Groans encircled the table.

"You know, *Captain*, if I didn't know better, I'd say you had an unfair home field advantage," Jack Stanton said.

Emil instantly shot an icy glare at him, and Jack wilted.

"It's a good thing I know better, right?" Jack said with a nervous chuckle. Emil mentally ordered his temper to stand down, and the game resumed. Two hands later, most of the chips sat in front of Emil. Scott Hauer yawned and stretched.

"Well, I've been fleeced," he said, glancing at Emil. "Time to go home and lie to my wife again."

Others around the table began to stir in agreement.

"Just a minute," Emil said. "I have a proposal for all of you gentlemen."

Eyebrows raised at both "proposal" and being called "gentlemen."

"Hold on to your wallet," Jack muttered.

"Nothing like that," Emil said. "How long have we been doing this?"

"Losing to you?" Scott joked.

"Playing poker together," Emil said, ignoring him.

"Five years," Jerry Laskey said.

"I propose we do something more productive with our Tuesday nights," Emil said.

They all waited for him to continue.

Emil looked around the table.

"Which of you is sick and tired of the inmates being treated like rock stars instead of the scum that they are?"

Every hand shot into the air.

"Good," Emil said. "I have a plan, but it hinges on total secrecy. No one can know about this little group and what it does. Are we agreed?"

Each set of eyes played around the room to another, asking a silent question. It was Jack who broke the silence.

"What would we be doing?"

"Well ..." Emil said, leaning in close to the group.

# TWENTY-FOUR

The din was louder than a packed stadium after a touchdown. Hundreds of inmates on cell block D screamed, chanted, and cheered as Leon made his way past them. His arms were raised, fists balled up as a symbol of victory. He bounced on the balls of his feet like a prizefighter after winning a championship bout.

Thousands of pieces of paper drifted slowly down. But this was no ticker tape parade. Leon's wrists were handcuffed, his feet in shackles. Four officers in riot gear escorted him as the cheering inmates showered him with torn up bits of toilet paper."

He had assaulted an officer and sent him to the hospital, and Leon was on his way to RHU again.

"What's the matter, you boys lost?" Leon said. "RHU is that way."

None of them responded. They continued their steady march down the hallway.

"What's up?" Leon laughed. "Did my early parole come through?"

They marched.

"Where the hell are you taking me?" he demanded, no longer feeling amused.

He knew if he went into some new solitary unit, he wouldn't get to act up for an audience of inmates in RHU. This he could not have. He tried to break away, but they held him in place. Again he tried, to no avail.

Finally, they stopped in front of door 114. They opened the door and led him in. It was a medium-sized gymnasium, with a single light hanging from the ceiling and a metal chair sitting in the middle of the room.

A twinge of fear ran down his neck at the sight of the chair.

"What's going on?" he demanded.

In answer, they dragged him to the chair. He struggled as much as he could in cuffs and shackles, but the most he managed was one solid kick landed on an officer's rib. He barely even flinched. With overwhelming strength and team effort, they sat him in the chair and hooked his restraints to a set of cuffs that was attached to a large metal ring attached to the chair. Once he was restrained, three of the officers left. One stood, staring down at him.

"We're doing things a little different from now on," the officer said. "Let me know if you like it."

Then he left, and Leon thought he heard the officer chuckle.

He sat there cuffed to the chair, in a poorly lit, empty room. The air had a stale, musty smell to it, as if the room hadn't been used for a long time.

He tried to identify the officers who brought him here, but couldn't.

They all wore riot gear, which concealed their features. Even the officer who had spoken to him had his voice muffled. As Leon pondered this, he heard light footsteps. They seemed odd, though, as if the person was shuffling.

*What kind of game are they playing now? Are they trying to make me think a zombie is coming to get me?*

He chuckled at the ridiculous thought, but it wouldn't

go away as the shuffling neared. He tried to keep panic out of his mind, but the unnerving thought wouldn't go away. As the form slowly made its way into the light, he could see the shape of an attractive woman's body. He sighed a breath of relief, chastising himself for such stupid fears.

"All right!" Leon said, smiling. "Maybe I will like this."

"I wouldn't be so sure," the woman said, with slightly slurred speech.

She stopped five feet from him, and he got a good look at her. From the right side, she looked like a beautiful woman. From the left was another story. She had a long, ugly scar running from what was left of her ear all the way down to her mouth. His face went from pleasure to confusion.

"What're you doing here?"

"Oh, good. You do remember me," she said with a grin that only showed on one side of her face. "Let's see if you remember this."

She pulled off her shirt.

"Do you remember what you did to me?" she said, running her fingers along a nasty scar that started at her shoulder, ran underneath her bra, and disappeared at the waistline of her jeans.

Then she took off her bra. One of her breasts was a thing of beauty, D-cup, firm, the perfect specimen. The other breast was just gone. In its place was the scar that ran from her shoulder, interrupted where a doctor had tried to sew a patch of skin over the opening.

Leon tried to look away, but she stepped towards him, grabbed his chin and turned his head back toward her.

"No, no, no." she said. "You don't get to turn away. I want you to remember this every time you think about grabbing that pathetic little pecker of yours."

He yanked his chin out of her hand.

"Are you done yet?"

"We haven't even started," she said with a smile that went from ear to scar. "You see, you took more from me than my looks and my acting career; you took my pride and self-worth."

"Boo freakin' hoo! What do you want, an apology? OK, I'm sorry you look like Frankenstein, how's that?"

She backed away and put her clothes back on. She laid her face in her palms.

"I just can't believe it," she said, making sobbing noises.

"Well, believe it," he said. "You drag your ugly ass down here thinking I would show some remorse? Please ... "

"No, I didn't think you would show remorse," she said, lifting her head, revealing her dry eyes and smiling face. "I can't believe you're this stupid."

It was the last thing he expected to hear. She reached behind her and pulled out a large survival knife.

"Recognize this? It's the knife you used on me."

She had his complete attention.

"Look," he said in a quiet voice, "I never meant to hurt you. I was drunk."

She leaned so close he could smell the alcohol on her breath.

"You think I would do this sober?" she said with a wicked grin.

"Do what?" he asked slowly.

"The same thing you did to me, for starters ... "

He began to struggle against his cuffs and shackles.

"Guard, Guard!" he screamed.

She laughed.

"Are you honestly calling for the people who brought you to me?" She chuckled. "Don't you think they knew what was going to happen?"

A cold sweat broke out on his face and neck.

"You can't do this." he screamed. "It's not legal!"

"Let's shut that mouth," she said, shoving the knife

through his cheek. "I'm sick of hearing it."

The four officers stood outside the door listening to the gurgled screams.

"It's about time," one of them said. "I thought she was going to lose her nerve."

"No," the tallest officer said. "You could see it in her eyes."

They listened to the screams rise and fall for over an hour.

Finally, there came a knock at the door. She stood, covered in blood, staring at her hands and shaking.

One officer escorted her to her car, while the others took what was left of Leon to the infirmary.

He lived for about an hour.

The infirmary staff was sworn to secrecy as to the identity of those involved. However, it didn't take long for the news to reach the grapevine that Leon was dead.

# TWENTY-FIVE

Two years after Leon's untimely death, Judge Bradley sat behind his bench in the Larsan County Courthouse and peered at the folder in front of him with disdain. He then looked over his glasses to the man standing in front of his desk with frustration. "Raymond Perry," he announced. "This is the fifth time you've been in my courtroom. Current charges are robbery, assault, and rape. I'm sentencing you to ten to twenty years at Larsan State Prison. Next case." Then he slammed his gavel down with the weight of a wasted lifetime behind it.

The next day, Raymond stepped off the bus with six other inmates newly sentenced to Larsan State Prison. He was not the most imposing figure, at five feet nine and 165 pounds. But he always liked to say, "The smallest dogs are the meanest."

He noticed a couple of officers looking at him and laughing. He made a mental note to get even. A large man stood in front of the six new inmates.

"I am Captain Sorn. You may call me 'Captain' or 'sir.' I am here to make sure that you parasites don't leave this facility until you have paid your debt to society. Even though we all know that society is better off without you.

This is not a playground; this is not a hotel. Treat the staff with respect, and you will be treated with respect. If you feel the need to misbehave," he paused and the air grew a few degrees colder as he lowered his voice to a menacing growl. "We have ways of dealing with that."

He marched them inside, where they were searched, showered, and issued inmate uniforms. Raymond and the other five were marched down the corridor of the main cell block.

He had been in other prisons before. The first walk to his cell was hellish. Prisoners screaming at him, coming on to him, throwing things at him. It was the inmates' little way of making him feel at home. But none of them had been like this.

As they trudged down the corridor, chills ran down Raymond's back. As quiet as it was, he expected to see a lot of empty cells. He was wrong. Each cell held two or more inmates. The prison was full, but none of the faces staring out at him made a sound. He tried to read the emotion in their eyes, but they all had a defeated, near-dead look. It was as if someone had stolen their heart and soul, and left the empty shells behind; like looking at a block full of corpses.

He had never seen anything like this before. He was terrified of what or who had done this, but he put on a brave face and acted like he was a kid walking to the candy store without a care in world.

When he reached his cell, the guard shoved him inside and slammed the cell door behind him. Raymond and his new cellmate to sized each other up, like two animals in the same cage.

His cellmate dwarfed him—he was six feet three and 225 pounds. He rose off the bed to tower over Raymond.

"Welcome to hell, little man. What did you do to deserve this place?"

Raymond smiled to hide the fear in his eyes. "What haven't I done, bro? Public enemy numero uno, right here."

Raymond thumped himself on the chest.

"Great," he said with an exasperated look. "So, you're a lifer, doing two to five years at a time. Figures I'd get stuck with you."

The man stared at him for a long moment. Raymond felt beads of sweat forming on his brow, unsure if the man had seen through his bravado.

The man held his gaze for a long moment, then shook his head in disgust and went back to his bunk.

Raymond let out a breath he didn't know he was holding and climbed into the top bunk.

"So, what do I call you?" Raymond tentatively asked.

No answer came for a long time, then finally he said, "Colton."

~

After settling in for a day or so, Raymond tried to get a feel for the place that was going to be his home for the next several years. Most of what he got was blank and angry stares. No one wanted to talk about it. This scared him even more. Someone always wanted to complain in prison.

~

One morning Raymond woke up, and things were louder than usual. Some inmates were even yelling. Raymond joined in, thinking, *Finally, some life in this place.*

"I wouldn't do that," Colton said. But Raymond ignored him. An officer walked by as Raymond was yelling.

"Is there a problem?"

"Who's talking to you, pig? Get out of here before I beat the crap out of you," Raymond said.

The guard reached into his pocket.

"What are you gonna do, pig? You gonna tase me? Just

try it. I'll sue you." The guard just pulled out a small notebook and wrote down Raymond's name and number, smiled at him, and then walked away.

Raymond stood there, shocked. Colton shook his head and went back to reading. The noise grew until the door to the cellblock opened and four officers in riot gear walked in. Instantly, the block became as silent as the grave.

People say only animals can smell fear, but you could sense it like the heaviness in the air before a storm. Raymond's hair stood on the back of his neck. The officers quietly marched down the tier. Inmates cringed and went to the back of their cells as the squad went past. Suddenly, they stopped in front of a cell.

The lead officer raised his hand, and the cell opened. The inmate inside was enormous, weighing nearly three hundred pounds of solid muscle. Raymond had seen him before. He seemed like a person no one wanted to mess with. However, when those four guards went into his cell, he started screaming and begging them not to take him.

After quite a fight, the officers managed to drag him out of the cellblock. His screams echoed down the corridor and faded into the distance.

"What a bunch of pansies," he said.

Colton stood, walked to Raymond, looked down at him, and said, "You'd better pray you never go through what he's about to."

"What? What do they go through? Visits with a counselor or pastor? Who cares?"

Colton shook his head and sat down on his bunk.

"Just keep watching," he said.

About an hour later, they dragged him back, unconscious and bleeding, and dumped him in his cell.

"What the hell?" Raymond whispered.

"I told you. You should just try to do your time quietly." Raymond stared at him in disbelief.

"Who took your balls?"

Colton pulled himself to full height, stared down at Raymond, and said, "You wanna say that again?"

"You see what those stinking guards did?"

Colton smiled.

"That would make it easy to get angry, wouldn't it? But the guards didn't do that."

"Who did then?"

"Pray you don't find out. What did you say your charges were?"

"Robbery, assault, rape," Raymond said, proudly.

"Ouch! Good luck with that."

~

So prison life went. Raymond tried to find out more about one-on-one visits, but no one was telling. It was like the entire prison had a code of silence about it.

*I'll find out, one way or another. I've got nothing but time,* he thought.

# TWENTY-SIX

One-on-ones. You could hear it being whispered throughout the block. The smell of fear was in the air. Raymond stood at his cell door to watch.

The door to the cellblock opened, and four officers in riot gear stepped onto the block. Raymond watched with morbid fascination to see who would be taken to "visits." He knew of a few inmates who were good candidates, always causing trouble. One by one, the squad passed their cells.

They came upstairs and started walking down Raymond's tier. A guard raised his hand, and Raymond's door opened. Too shocked to react, they quickly cuffed Raymond and dragged him out.

"We hear you've been asking questions about one-on-one visits," the officer said. "We'll be more than happy to show you what they're all about."

Then they took him to a room he had never seen before. The number on the door was 114. A guard inserted a key into the lock and turned it. The door opened into a large, dark room. "What is this place," Raymond muttered.

They sat him down and cuffed him to a small metal chair. He braced himself for a beating, but to his surprise they left the room.

He looked around. There were dents in the floor and walls that didn't look like they belonged there. In several places were red spots. *Dried blood?* he wondered. He felt another presence in the room.

Someone came toward him out of the darkness. Raymond squinted to see who it was. Raymond recognized him. It was the man he had assaulted.

"Why are you here?" Raymond asked.

The man smiled, but in his eyes there was something more than happiness, something dark.

"Justice," he said, and then he pulled a baseball bat from behind his back. It was the same baseball bat that Raymond had used to beat him so badly that he'd been sent to the hospital. Raymond's eyes widened in fear as the realization struck him right before the bat did. The officers in the hallway smiled as they listened to Raymond's muffled screams for mercy.

After twenty minutes, the shrieks and shouts of rage abated. The civilian walked out covered in blood, with a haunted look in his eyes like he had just lost a part of his soul. The officers had seen it dozens of times before. Victims came in thirsting for vengeance and left looking hollow and unsatisfied.

The officers escorted him out and then came back and take what was left of the inmate to the infirmary.

Raymond woke up two days later. The nurse told him he had a concussion and three broken ribs. He would be there for at least a week. As he panned around the room, he saw that the infirmary had lots of beds, but none were empty.

Raymond's time in the infirm crawled by. There was no TV, no games, nothing to pass the time. The only distraction was when someone left and someone new came in. The beds were never empty for long. As soon as someone left, his space was taken. Sometimes they didn't even stop at a bed. The nurses would check those unfortunate ones and call a doctor to pronounce him dead.

Raymond lay mercifully asleep. Sleep had fought him for days, like a prizefighter unwilling to give up his belt. But tonight Raymond had finally won.

He dreamed about driving down the road with the window down, the radio playing his favorite song. He pulled into a roadside drive-in diner. A pretty, young waitress in a tight, pink miniskirt and white halter top skated up to his window and leaned down. Her halter barely covered her large breasts, and when she bent over to take his order, Raymond was hard pressed to keep his eyes away from her cleavage.

"You see anything you like, sugar?" she said with a wink and a smile.

Raymond was dragged back to consciousness as another inmate was brought into the infirm, screaming, blood pouring out of his severed leg. The lower half had been completely detached and was lying on the gurney beside him as though it had been tossed there as an afterthought.

The screams continued as they wheeled him into another room. For hours, shrieks of pain escaped the back room, until they were suddenly silenced. Whether he was sedated or dead, Raymond never knew, but he never saw that inmate again.

He tried to return to his dream, but once again, sleep avoided him. As he lay there, his own injuries started hurting again. With nothing else to do but lie in pain, Raymond became acutely aware of the smells of the infirm. The sweating, injured bodies, mixed with the smell of disinfectant and death haunted him.

Two days before, the inmate in the cot next to him had

died during the night. The nurses didn't find out until several hours later. The stench of death still weighed heavily on Raymond's mind. He vowed that he would find a way out of this nightmare.

He healed enough to limp back to his old cell. The door to his cell slammed shut, reverberating through his pounding head. Thirteen days of hell healing in the infirmary, and now he was back in his cell. He loathed to think of it as home, but it was better than the medical wing.

He was tired and just wanted to go to sleep, but his top bunk seemed like it was a mile in the air. He tried several times to get his mattress up on the bunk, but with his ribs wrapped, and still feeling the effects of the concussion, every failed attempt was a new adventure in pain.

Finally, he collapsed to the floor, crawled to his mattress, and lay there. His cellmate came back from rec an hour later and nearly tripped over him.

"Raymond, are you OK?"

Raymond looked up at him from where he was lying and said, "No."

Colton looked down and made a decision. He grabbed his own mattress and put it on the top bunk. Then he put Raymond's mattress on the bottom. He gently helped Raymond into the lower bunk.

"Thank you, Colton," Raymond said. Then he painfully rolled over and fell into a fitful sleep.

A look of concern and even guilt flashed across Colton's face. He opened his mouth as if to say something but then closed it again.

# TWENTY-SEVEN

Raymond no longer exhibited any desire to instigate trouble or call attention to himself. He worked hard to blend into the background, rising at once for every count, following every rule, doing everything by the book. He didn't want to risk another trip to Room 114.

Officers on their rounds found him compliant. When they made eye contact, he acknowledged their authority with a nod, but he never smiled, never spoke, only cringed on the inside.

Colton noticed how quiet Raymond had become.

"It's interesting, isn't it?" Colton said.

"What?"

"How sometimes fear can have its own smell."

"Like urine?"

"Sometimes. When one-on-ones start, you can smell it. Sometimes it's so thick you can almost feel it, like the heaviness in the air before a storm."

"I feel it every time," Raymond whispered.

"Now do you understand? They keep us in line through fear."

"Have you ever been there?"

"Where?"

Raymond shuddered involuntarily as he said, "The room."

Colton paused for a moment as if carefully considering how to answer, then he simply said, "No."

"You're lucky."

Then Raymond drifted off to sleep.

~

Time heals all wounds. Not completely. There will always be a scar, but the wound becomes less painful as time goes on.

After a while, Raymond's fear started to fade, as the memory of the horror wasn't as fresh in his mind. What he found was that others who had gone through "visits" formed a sort of twisted fraternity.

Winter began to exert its will over fall. The cold seeped in through the concrete walls and wouldn't leave. It was as though winter itself had become an unwelcome visitor.

The first snowfall made everything look beautiful, but it only made the inmates think of where else they would rather be. With a change in the weather, sickness was on the rise. Colton came down with a nasty case of bronchitis. There was little Raymond could do but watch his friend suffer.

Raymond repeatedly asked for medical to check Colton out. They quickly examined him once and said he just had a chest cold. After that, they didn't do anything, no matter how much Raymond begged.

He was getting sick and tired of seeing neglect and injustice in this place. The only thing they weren't slack on was discipline. Aside from one on ones, the prison was very strict. If you stepped one toe out of line, they dealt with you swiftly and brutally.

Raymond sat on his bunk leaning against the cold

concrete wall. He threw another card onto the bed, and Colton quickly picked it up.

"Hey, Colt, who started all this brutal discipline crap? I've never seen a prison that had it this bad."

"You don't want to go there," Colton said, stifling a cough.

"Why not?"

Colton threw out a card. "You've seen how brutal this place is, and you still have to ask that question?"

"The walls don't have ears, do they?"

"Yes."

"Sometimes I just don't get you, man. Don't you want someone to treat your sickness?"

"Yes, but it won't happen that way."

"So, you'll just suffer through, is that it?"

"There really isn't any other option."

"Yes, there is. There's got to be. Somebody's got to pay for this."

"Don't do it," Colton said, picking up another card.

"Do what?"

"Drive yourself crazy like this again. There's nothing you can do to stop it, and if you try ... well, you know what happens."

Raymond involuntarily shuddered. He looked over at Colton, studying his cards.

"Gin," Colton said.

"How can you do that, man?"

"Do what? I filled my hand with a run."

"I mean just sit there with all the injustice going on around you and do nothing."

"Forgive and forget. That's what I'm told to do," he said picking up his Bible.

"Isn't there something in there about helping the downtrodden, or something like that?"

Colton smiled. "I think there is."

"So that's it; you have to help me. We have to rescue the downtrodden and lead them to the promised land."

Colton smiled.

"Which promised land is that?"

"The promised land of getting out early and suing the state."

"Not good enough," Colton chuckled.

Raymond stared him right in the eye.

"How about you not dying from medical neglect?"

"I'll be OK," Colton said, stifling another cough.

"How about the promised land of the lives you could save? Of the people who are being punished twice for the same thing? Is that good enough for you?"

"Why do you care?" Colton asked. "What happened to Mr. 'I'm a rebel. You can't hold me down?'"

"He got some sense beat into him," Raymond said.

"I'll help you. If you can answer me one question. Why are you doing this, really? Is it to stop them from hurting anyone else? Or is it for your own vengeance?"

"A little bit of both."

"Not good enough. If you do it for revenge then you're no better than they are, and where does the cycle end?"

"How do you figure that?"

"If you get revenge on the officers, then their families will want revenge on you, and it never stops. The question is, do you want to be part of the problem, or part of the solution?"

Raymond was quiet for a moment. The wheels in his mind turned the conversation over and over, examining it from every angle.

"Part of the solution."

"Then you have to do it for the right reasons."

"Fine, I'll be a good boy," Raymond said in mock disgust.

Colton grinned.

"The trick is to prove that there was any wrongdoing."

"What about the injuries, the deaths?"

Colton shook his head.

"The word of a convicted felon will never hold up in court. There're too many other ways those injuries could've occurred, especially in a prison. Any jury would see that as a desperate attempt to get money or a shorter sentence."

"How dare they question our purely humanitarian motives," Raymond said, with a sly grin.

# TWENTY-EIGHT

Raymond applied for a trustee job and was given cleanup duty on the daytime cleaning crew. Colton didn't understand why he would sign up for such a busy job.

"I just wanted to get a good look at that secretary," Raymond said.

Colton eyed him dubiously.

"You've been in prison for how long?"

"About seven months."

"I'd have to be here for twenty years to be interested in that secretary."

Raymond smiled. "Don't worry, I've got it under control."

"I hope you know what you're doing."

"Trust me."

Patrice Wilkins was an overly large woman. "Big-boned," she would say, but nobody gained ten pounds of bone after a weekend eating binge. Patrice had an eating problem. But like everyone else with a problem, she turned a blind eye to it.

Aside from being overweight, Patrice also was not overly blessed with good looks. Having a mustache that needed to be shaved every day didn't help either. What she lacked in all those areas she more than made up for in bust size.

Because of this alone, she still got looks of desire from the inmates. This made her feel like she was a major hottie. Patrice put on the image of disdaining inmates, but in reality, she was not above trading affection for things the inmates needed.

More than a few inmates were called to the office under the ruse of discipline, only to have Patrice lock the door behind them. Each of left with whatever thing they needed and a haunted look on their face. Patrice never had repeat customers.

Raymond had a hard time adjusting to the new job.

"Are you sure it's worth this?" Colton asked.

"Yes."

He was still hurting from his injuries from the one-on-one, but he couldn't show he was in pain. Trustee jobs in a prison are hard to come by and in great demand. They allow an inmate a measure of freedom while paying them a pittance, usually around fifty cents an hour. It may not be much, but it's enough for them to order stamps, envelopes, snacks from the inmate commissary. The downside of such labor is they don't tolerate calling off sick. If he asked for a break or a day off, they would just fire him. Dozens of inmates were begging for jobs. So he had to suck it up and keep his mouth shut.

He was waiting for "that moment."

Unfortunately, that moment took months to make itself available. They worked him hard all day cleaning bathrooms, waxing and buffing floors, and whatever else needed doing.

He went over his plan every day. It was simple enough. All outgoing mail was searched for contraband to make sure no sensitive information left the prison. After it was searched, the secretary would seal it and send it out on the mail truck.

An inmate worker would haul the mailbags out to the truck, the mail carrier would inspect them, then take them to the post office for processing. All Raymond had to do was get a letter out without Patrice reading it.

Raymond replayed his plan in his mind. He would approach her—whom he had been flirting with for the last month—and tell her that he forgot to mail a letter to his mom, and it was her birthday tomorrow.

The real letter, which he would have to find a way to switch, started with, "Dear Tony, I'm calling in a favor. I need you to take this letter to the police."

He was starting to wonder if this was worth all the trouble, when his moment finally came.

The mail was running a little late, and Patrice asked Raymond if he could take the bag to the mailroom.

"I'm not sure if I'm allowed," Raymond said, trying not to seem too eager.

"Do it just this one time, as a favor to me?" she said.

Raymond paused. "I don't think I should," he said, then started to walk away.

"I'm sure there's something I could do for you," she said seductively.

Raymond suppressed a shudder.

"Actually, there is. I have a letter I didn't get in the mail on time, and it's for my mother. If I don't get it out today, I'll miss getting it to her on her birthday."

"You know I can't add mail to the bags without checking it."

"Check away," he said, handing her the letter.

She checked it quickly, saw that there was nothing hidden in it, and put it back in the envelope without reading it.

"Are you sure that's all I can do for you?"

Fighting not to show how much he wanted to vomit at the thought, he just smiled.

"I'll take these letters to the mail room, thanks." Then he hefted the bags onto his shoulders and left.

On the way to the delivery bay was a small hallway that was seldom used. Raymond pretended to need a rest to put down the bags. He quickly replaced the letter with the one that he intended to go out and resealed the envelope.

"What are you doing here?" an officer demanded, as Raymond picked up the bags.

"I needed a little rest. These things are heavy."

"What's in your hand?"

Raymond looked down at the letter in his hand. Quickly, he remembered the cover story that he had practiced for weeks.

"It fell out of one of the bags."

The guard eyed him suspiciously. He looked at the letter. It was sealed and stamped "approved." The officer stared at the letter. Raymond suddenly dropped both bags at his feet.

"These bags are heavy. If you want to search that letter, you can take it to the delivery bay when you're done," he said.

Raymond held his breath mentally, waiting to see if his gamble would pay off or backfire.

"Here!" the officer said, throwing the letter at Raymond. "Get these bags out of my hallway."

He quickly stuffed the letter deep into the bag, where even he couldn't have found it. Then he hoisted the bags again and started toward the mail room.

The bags seemed to feel lighter. He was sure it was just the mental weight that had lifted. After dropping them off, he had to keep himself calm. Skipping back to his cell would be a dead giveaway that he had just sent the letter that could tear this prison apart and end one-on-ones.

# TWENTY-NINE

Joe sat down for his morning cup of coffee. In twelve years as a police officer, he had never missed a cup. This morning he opened the mail piled in his inbox, as he added cream and half a sugar, stirring as he read a letter that had been forwarded to him from the Larsan County Sheriff's Department. He finished stirring, and raised the Styrofoam cup to his lips, but didn't drink. The letter disturbed him so much that he put his coffee down and went in search of a familiar face. He stopped in front of the desk of a man in his early forties with a graying ponytail, black jeans, biker boots, and a Metallica T-shirt. The man was leaning back in his chair, wearing dark sunglasses.

"You need to see this," Joe said without looking up from the letter.

The man's only response was a mild snore. Joe gave a knowing sigh followed by a mischievous grin. He leaned in close so that his mouth was right next to the sleeping man's ear.

"Oh, baby, last night was fantastic," he whispered in his best imitation of a woman's seductive voice. "How about again this morning?"

The man slowly began to stir.

"OK, baby," he whispered while yawning. "I can be a little late for work."

He rolled his head toward the voice and opened his eyes. Joe hadn't moved, and the shock of seeing Joe's smiling face next to his sent him reeling, nearly falling out of his chair.

"What's wrong with you, man? Give me a freakin' heart attack."

Joe laughed so hard he had to lean on the desk to steady himself.

"That wasn't cool, man."

"I owed you that."

"For what?"

"Let's see, how about the used chewing gum in my coffee last week?"

"Oh, um ... "

"Or my stapler that mysteriously got glued to my computer monitor two months ago?"

"Um ... "

"Or the toilet paper incident?"

"I told you, I had nothing to do with that. I don't know where that crowbar came from."

"Uh-huh."

The man suddenly tried his best to look like he was swamped with work. "Did you come here for a reason? I'm very busy."

"Yeah, I saw how busy you were, inspecting the insides of your eyelids. Is today dress-down day?"

"Didn't you get the memo?"

Joe turned serious. "So, how was last night?"

"Well, you know how boring stakeouts are?"

"Of course."

"Undercover stakeouts are ten times worse."

"Did you find anything?"

"Nothing. Wasted trip."

"I've got another one for you."

## CHAPTER 29

"Great," the man in the Metallica shirt said with mock enthusiasm.

"Read this."

He took the letter, read a little, and said, "So? It needs to be investigated, but why me?"

"Read the name of the one causing the trouble."

"Oh, no."

"Now do you understand?"

"I'll get right on it," he said earnestly.

~

Sam Smythe arrived at Larsan Prison to no fanfare, no special greeting, nothing out of the ordinary, but he was the immediate focus of the entire prison. At 5'10", 160 pounds, he was not an imposing man, but he had a spark of intelligence in his eye and something about him that said, "I don't belong here." He was a quiet, respectful man in his forties, with graying hair that had recently been cut. He did not speak unless he had to and gave no one any reason to dislike him. Naturally, everyone hated and/or feared him.

The officers all thought he was from Internal Affairs. The inmates all thought he was a cop. He was very observant of little things and made notes for himself that he showed no one. The first time he 'fell' in the rec yard, he spent a week in the infirm. The second time, it was closer to two. He never complained, though. He still kept to his same routine as though nothing had happened. It unnerved his cellmate, a large man who just happened to be in with the inmates who had beaten Sam.

Raymond had heard rumors of an undercover cop being in Larsan and tried to talk to Sam secretly. But Sam wasn't interested. He lived in his own world and treated everyone else as neighbors that he really didn't want to talk to.

Colton told Raymond to leave Sam alone. "He just has a

funny air about him. I can't place my finger on it, but something isn't right."

Raymond, however, was convinced Sam was a cop and kept trying to pass information to him.

Emil told his officers to steer clear of Sam.

"If he's IA we'll find out soon enough. Don't give him any ammunition to use against you."

One day, Sam's cellmate wasn't up for count. In fact, he wasn't there at all. The officers searched through the count sheets and found that through one mistake or another, he had missed three counts, which meant he had been gone for nearly twenty-four hours. Sam was questioned thoroughly but claimed to know nothing. When the cellmate's property was searched, they found detailed escape plans. Emil was enraged.

Within hours, Sam found himself in room 114. Emil stormed down the hallway toward the room, with an officer running beside him, trying to keep up.

"Sir, are you sure you want to do this?"

"Yes!" Emil snapped back.

"But what if he really is IA?"

"I don't care. Nobody escapes from my prison!"

He blasted the door open, nearly flattening the officer standing behind it.

"Where is he?" he screamed in Sam's face.

"Where is who? Sam asked.

His answer was a vicious right smashing the side of his face. Sam shook his head, spat out blood and a tooth, and then looked back at Emil and smiled.

"How am I supposed to talk if you break my jaw?"

Emil stood somewhere between rage and astonishment at his nonchalance.

"Are you a cop?"

Sam lowered his head until Emil could only see half of his eyes.

The dark orbs gazed at him with bridled malevolence.

"Captain Sorn, does it bother you to know that you might not be in control of the situation? Has the hunter become the prey? Do you feel the cold perspiration of fear running down the back of your neck?"

"I asked you a question. Are you a cop? You know you have to answer."

"Or what? I'll get in trouble?" Sam asked. "I'm cuffed to a chair in an empty room. I assume that camera doesn't work, and I have a psychotic egomaniac who's strong as an ox beating the hell out of me. Did I miss anything? I don't think I can get into much more trouble than that."

Emil reached behind him, pulled out a large kitchen knife and showed it to Sam.

"Are you a cop?"

"Define 'cop.'"

"Are you involved with any type of law enforcement?"

"Are you?"

"You know I am."

"Then I suppose I am too."

Emil backed down a little. "Where is your cellmate? Did you help him escape?"

Sam thought for a moment. "I know where he is, and I suppose you could say I helped him escape ... a little bit."

"So how did you avoid the nighttime count?"

"I told the officer that he was working late getting ready for breakfast tomorrow."

"And he believed you?"

"He walked away mumbling something about always being the last to know."

"Which officer?"

"Sorry, people in uniform all look alike to me."

"You know you'll get charges for this."

"No, I don't think I will."

"How are you planning on getting away with that?"

"By naming my accomplices."

Emil pulled out a pen and paper. "OK, who are they?"

"You."

"Funny. Now, who are they?"

"You, every officer and inmate who ate lunch. That's around what; twelve-hundred accomplices?"

Emil slowly put the pen and paper away.

"Each and every one of you helped him escape." Sam looked thoughtful for a moment. "You could say you ate him out of house and home."

"Where is he?" Emil demanded.

"How about a riddle?"

"What?"

"Down a slippery slope I go, into a pool that waits below. Squeeze myself through hollow tube, though nostrils close and senses swoon. I crawl through muck, I cannot see. On for miles and then I'm free."

Emil smiled. "Thank you." Emil turned to an officer and said, "He's in the sewer."

"You could say that," Sam said. "What did you have for lunch today, Captain?"

Emil eyed him suspiciously.

"Cheeseburger and fries, just like everyone else."

"How did it taste?"

"Not bad," Emil said, concerned with the direction this conversation was heading.

"That's good. A cook always likes to hear that his meal is appreciated. But I digress. In the end, you helped my cellmate escape more than I did, you see. I had a salad today for lunch," Sam said, leveling his gaze at Emil.

"Impossible. I didn't help him at all."

"On the contrary, let's just say that today, they should change the name from hamburgers to Victorburgers," Sam said, with a smug look plastered on his face.

Realization dawned on Emil slowly.

"You didn't."

"Of course I did," Sam said. "The man was a pig, so I butchered him."

Emil took a step back without realizing it. "How?"

"It wasn't hard. We both worked in the kitchen. I gave him a little something to make him sick. He told the cook, and she sent him back to his cell. Before he left, though, I asked him to help me get a box off a high shelf in the freezer. While his back was turned, I smashed his skull with a frozen turkey, stacked some boxes in front of him, and left him to freeze to death.

"Later, when I was sent to grind some meat for the hamburgers, I had a certain lump of meat in mind. I had to cut him into manageable sections, but he ground up very nicely, I think."

Emil looked at him in sheer horror. The officer standing guard at the door vomited.

"Go check this out with the cook," Emil told the officer. He took a moment to compose himself before continuing to question Sam.

Sam started laughing hysterically as the officer returned. Emil turned away in disgust and went to meet the officer.

"The cook confirmed that inmate Victor took off work yesterday."

A cold fire burned in Emil's eyes. He walked back over to Sam, who was still laughing, put the knife to Sam's throat, and said, "You sick ..."

The last word was smothered by the gurgle of Sam's throat being sliced open as blood sprayed. His eyes went wild as he struggled against his cuffs.

"Sir? Are you all right?"

Emil grinned just a little.

"Maybe the kitchen will serve Sam-wiches for lunch today."

The officer considered telling his superior what a lousy

comedian he would make, but seeing Emil holding the bloody knife, looking every bit as deranged as Sam, silenced him.

# THIRTY

Summer came early to Larsan Prison that year, with temperatures averaging eighty degrees throughout May. Oddly, this prompted most of the experienced officers to wear their long-sleeve uniforms to work. The reason was the heating/air conditioning system. Fifteen years earlier, the state had a budget surplus, so the warden used this opportunity to replace their old system, which was barely big enough to handle the prison's needs. The maintenance supervisor, who had only been on the job six months, overestimated the size of the units they would need. As a result, the hotter it got outside, the colder it got inside. When the thermometer reached one hundred, you could build a snowman in the main block. Consequently, if the temperature hit zero outside, you could almost smell the flesh cooking. Inmates would sleep on the floor, just to feel the cool concrete.

One hot day in mid-June, the bus pulled up carrying new inmates as usual, with Emil standing by. As they stepped off the bus, the last inmate looked at Emil with recognition and actually smiled. Emil recognized him but did not return the smile. After they had been processed and assigned housing, Emil escorted the familiar inmate to his cell. The inmate put his things down and turned to talk to Emil.

"Do you recognize me?" the inmate asked.

"Harley Richardson, right?"

"Yep. It's been a few years."

"Around twenty."

"I just wanted to say thanks. If it wasn't for you, I never would've graduated," Harley said with a smile.

"I see it did you a lot of good," Emil answered with a face of stone.

"Yeah, I guess I messed up."

"No, they don't send people here who 'mess up.' They only send us hard-core criminals. So, don't try to play the old-school-buddy routine with me. It won't work out well for you, understand?"

Harley stood back and gave a mock salute.

"Yes, sir!"

Emil turned and walked away. Harley called after him.

"Hey, Emil, it's good to see you finally grew a set of balls."

Emil stopped, pulled out his notebook, jotted down Harley's name, smiled at him and walked away.

"Not smart," said an inmate three cells down.

"We're old school pals. I'm just messin' with him," Harley said.

"I'll guarantee you he doesn't see it that way."

"Oh, well, then he can't take a joke. What's he gonna do?"

"You don't wanna know."

Every time Harley saw Emil, he would pick on him or call him by his first name. Harley was having fun. One night he lay in bed sleeping, when his cell popped open, and guards with flashlights grabbed him. They cuffed him and dragged him kicking and screaming to room 114. They cuffed him to the metal chair and left. Harley looked around the large, sparsely lit room and locked his eyes on Emil walking toward him out of the darkness.

"It appears we have a problem, you and I," Emil said, while twirling his nightstick absently. Harley's eyes locked on the weapon.

"I assume this isn't a social call," Harley said with a nervous chuckle. His laughter was cut short by the whistle-crack of the nightstick smashing into his skull, causing him to buckle in pain.

"I let you have the first comment because we used to be friends, and it was your first day."

The weapon crashed savagely into his leg, with a satisfying crack.

"But you kept pushing it." Emil dealt him a blow to the ribs.

"I have worked too hard getting these inmates in line to let you mess it up." The weapon smashed into his face, breaking his nose and sending blood flying.

"From now on, you will address me as 'Captain' or 'sir.' Any comments from my past will end, and you will be a model inmate for the remainder of your stay."

He hovered over Harley's bleeding, barely conscious body. Emil pulled his chin up with the nightstick.

"Is that understood?"

Harley nodded.

"Good. Just to be sure you got the message, though ... "

Emil swung with vicious fury, connecting with Harley's skull, sending him into unconsciousness and splintering the nightstick.

Harley spent the next few weeks in the infirmary recuperating. He passed the time asking other inmates about their injuries. No one felt like talking much, but he managed to dig up a little information.

~

Raymond felt great on one hand. His letter would chip away at the foundation of this place, and with any luck, it would crumble. On the other hand, Raymond was terrified that the letter had somehow fallen into the wrong hands. He became edgy, even jumpy. Then he started losing sleep over it, and fear turned into paranoia. He became convinced that the captain knew about the letter.

"I'm going to die in the chair; I just know it," Raymond said.

"What makes you think that?'

"I don't know, man. I just have this feeling that I can't shake."

"Look, you've been doing good, laying low, staying off the radar, I think if you keep that up you'll be fine."

"I'm done with this place, man. I'm makin' a run."

Colton's hand quickly clamped over Raymond's mouth, and he whispered, "You never, ever say that out loud."

Raymond jerked away from him.

"Get off me!" They stared at each other.

"You'll never make it," Colton said.

"I've got to try. I can't live in fear of my next 'visit' for the next twenty years."

"If you get caught, you'll wish you were never born."

"There're times I wish that now," Raymond said.

"So why do you want to take the risk?" Colton asked. "I need a better answer than, 'just because.'"

Raymond lowered his head. For a long time, silence reigned in the cell. Colton thought he had fallen asleep, but then he slowly spoke.

"Every night I dream the same dream," Raymond said, hesitating. "I'm sent to room 114 to clean up a mess. As I step into the room, the stench of death assaults my senses. I make my way across the floor that is slippery with blood. On the way, I gather a severed arm and leg and throw them into a large trash bag like used tissues to be thrown away.

Mopping up the blood, I'm struck by how commonplace this seems, as though it happens every day, like cleaning a toilet. I work my way toward a bloody torso, which, for some reason, still has the head attached. I clean up around the chair, telling myself not to look at the face. I almost make it. As I slide the torso into a large trash bag, I catch a glimpse of the face. I freeze. Not only does the face reveal the incredible pain and fear of this poor creature's last moments, but it reveals something else.

"It's my face staring back at me through dead eyes. I awake from this dream, stifling a scream, drenched in sweat. This dream has plagued me ever since the day I saw the room for myself."

The cell was silent, as Colton allowed the story to sink in.

Colton eyed Raymond as if reassessing him. "OK, I'll help you, on one condition. My name never gets mentioned, you understand me?"

"Absolutely!"

# THIRTY-ONE

Once Raymond started concentrating on planning the escape, his paranoia subsided. He transferred from day to nighttime cleaner. He worked hard for two months before he even started to concoct his plan. He thought that would draw away any suspicions. He was right. A few of the night shift officers got to know him by name and even trust him a little. He was friendly and joked with them, always careful to keep things on a professional level. He never asked for favors, always addressed the officers as "sir," and treated them with respect.

He studied their habits looking for weaknesses and tendencies. Each morning he shared his observations of the previous night with Colton. Slowly, a plan began to form. Colton started giving Raymond specific questions to ask certain officers—never more than two per night—to avoid arousing suspicion. He also gave Raymond particular jokes to tell the officers, and they kept track of the responses.

They noted, in code, what officer worked what shift on what day. They drew a picture of a dream house. They colored and decorated it and even labeled the living room, bedroom, and kitchen, but it was actually an elaborate map of the prison concealed inside the picture. If you ignored the colors, you could see all the routes out of the prison.

They started collecting supplies and hiding them in the cleaning supply closet. They had all the plans and materials they needed in place, when one day they got hit with a surprise cell search. Theirs was the only cell searched on the entire block.

Raymond and Colton looked at each other and exchanged a silent thought.

*They know.*

Two officers searched the cell, while a third kept an eye on the inmates. Raymond and Colton tried to remain as cool as possible pretending that they didn't even care that their cell was being searched. The officers were serious about their work. Blankets, sheets, and mattresses flew off the bunks. They rifled through papers and threw them aside. When the officer in charge came across the drawing of the house, Colton held his breath.

"Who drew this?" the officer asked.

Colton responded.

"Whose property are you tearing through?" he said.

"That's what I'm asking," said the officer.

"Well, since you pigs are determined to destroy what little we have, I couldn't tell you right now whose is whose."

Raymond looked from officer to officer, judging their reactions. Colton was right; the room did look like a tornado had landed right in the middle. The officer approached Colton.

"I was gonna say 'nice drawing,' but instead …" He ripped the picture into shreds and flushed it down the toilet. "That was for 'pigs.' You have a nice day." The officer bumped his shoulder on the way out of the cell.

"Hey, are you going to clean this up?" Colton yelled at the backs of the officers. They pretended not to hear him.

Raymond looked at his cellmate and whispered, "What

the hell is wrong with you? Why would you piss them off while they're searching our cell?"

"Because if I didn't object, they'd know something was up. And because he had found the map. Once it became an issue of defiance, he lost interest in the search."

"Very impressive, but we lost the map."

"It doesn't matter. You've studied it enough. You'll do fine."

Raymond wished that he felt as confident as Colton sounded.

They waited another month. Finally, their day came. Officer Okrie was working in central, Stevens was the officer on their block, and Stroe was the hallway officer. Raymond had to fight hard to contain his excitement. Colton calmed him down by telling him he would blow the whole thing if he didn't cool off.

They went over the plan twice, double-checked that Raymond had everything, and knew what to say. When they were done, they shredded everything that had anything to do with the plan and flushed it.

Raymond said to Colton, "Thanks, man. I couldn't have gotten this far without you."

"Just remember our deal," Colton said. "My name doesn't get mentioned."

"Absolutely."

Time seemed like it was mired in mud that evening. When Officer Stevens finally came to get Raymond for his work shift, he found the inmate 'asleep,' and jostled him 'awake.' Raymond apologized and told the officer that he wasn't feeling well but would try to do his cleaning duties. Stevens handed Raymond off to Stroe, the hallway officer, who took him to the cleaning closet to get his cart.

His first job was to empty trash cans. Once they were done, they took the bags out the back door and threw them in the Dumpster. On the way back inside, the real plan began. Fifteen years ago, all the locks on the doors in the corridors and the back door had been changed from-deadbolt style, where you had to relock them with a key, to a beveled latch, which would automatically lock when the door shut. Eventually, the officers grew complacent, not bothering to make sure the doors actually locked when they slammed shut. Raymond used this to his advantage. Before they went out the back door, Raymond told officer Stroe a riddle.

"A cowboy rides into town on Friday, stays three days, and leaves on Friday. How did he do it?"

Stroe was still thinking about it when they came back in from dumping the trash and didn't notice Raymond placing a small strip of metal over the back-door latch.

*So far, so good.*

They went back through the corridors, with Stroe not even noticing that Raymond was the last one through each door. He was too busy trying to get clues about the riddle.

"Did he have a time machine?" Stroe asked.

"This ain't *Back to the Future*. He's just a plain old cowboy," Raymond said.

"Was he a twin?"

"What? No, a cowboy, not two cowboys."

"What town was he in?"

"That doesn't matter."

"I'm gonna get this, even if it kills me."

They got back to the cleaning closet. Raymond filled his mop bucket and started mopping the halls. Stroe tried one last time to answer the riddle.

"The calendar was shorter back then, and the weeks only had three days."

"That was pretty lame. I'll tell you when I'm done mopping," Raymond promised, as Stroe went off to take his break.

Raymond mopped the main hallway, as usual. He put

out the "wet floor" signs, then put his mop and bucket away, took a swallow of cleaning solution, knowing he would be cleaning his cellblock next. He had tried this once before, and knew it only took about two minutes to kick in. By the time Raymond got to his cellblock he was greener than a Granny Smith apple. Officer Stevens was not the most diligent officer in some respects, but he took great pride in having his uniform pressed and always looking immaculate.

"Sir, I really don't feel well. Could I go back to my cell?" Raymond asked.

Stevens eyed him skeptically.

"Did you get all your work done?"

"No, sir. I got the trash out, and the main hallway …"

Then, midsentence, it hit. Raymond couldn't have stopped it if he wanted to. He projectile vomited all over Officer Stevens. The officer just sat there staring at his soiled uniform and desk in shock.

"I'm so very sorry, sir. Here, let me help you," Raymond said and tried to wipe off some of the vomit. Stevens drew back like he was going to hit Raymond, but instead he punched a button to his cell, and said through gritted teeth, "Go … to … your … cell!"

Raymond obeyed, as Stevens walked to the officers' changing room. Back at Raymond's cell, Colton was waiting, holding the cell door open.

"How's it going?"

"Perfect, so far."

He changed out of his soiled clothes and headed back out of the cell, pausing to look back and say, "Thanks again … for everything."

"Good luck. I'll see you on the outside someday."

Raymond gave a quick nod and stepped out of the cell.

# THIRTY-TWO

Raymond walked briskly past the deserted post where vomit was still lying on the desk and into the corridor. This was the dangerous part. Officer Okrie was posted in central, where all the camera monitors were. Central was supposed to monitor any inmate movement. Officer Okrie had a bad (or in Raymond's case *good*) habit of falling asleep partway into his shift. The catch was, Raymond had no way of knowing if he was asleep or awake. He would just have to act as though he was doing his normal cleaning routine.

He opened the first door and retrieved the piece of metal, so the door latched shut. Now he was committed. After the second door, he got his mop and bucket and took it with him. The third door stuck a little, causing a mild panic. He knew precious seconds were ticking away, and each one was that much closer to alarms going off. His panic blossomed when he tried again and the door still wouldn't open. Sweat popped out on his forehead, and streamed down his cheeks. He could feel the unblinking eye of the security camera staring a hole in his back. He could almost hear it laughing at him, taunting him, 'Hey boy. What are you doing out of your cell?'

He took one of the other pieces of metal and frantically

shoved against the door. Mercifully, it sprung open. He rounded the corner heading for the back door, just as Officer Stroe came back from his break to an empty hallway. Stroe knew that Raymond wouldn't shirk his duties, so he went to check on him. When he got to Raymond's block, Officer Stevens was still cleaning his desk.

"Have you seen Raymond? He's not in the hallway?" Stroe said.

Stevens shot him a look of death.

"Yes, I've seen the SOB. He's in his cell."

"What happened?"

"He puked all over me, that's what happened," Stevens yelled.

Stroe stifled a laugh.

"Well, he did say he was feeling sick. Have you checked on him?"

"No!"

"I'll go take a look, to see if he's OK," Stroe said.

The smell of vomit slapped him in the face before he made it to Raymond's cell. Stroe swallowed hard to keep from gagging and peered into the cell. A blanket covered figure huddled in Raymond's bunk; the stench was even harsher, if that was possible."

"Raymond?" he whispered, but got no response. "Raymond?" he said a little louder. No answer except a low moan. He couldn't tell if it had come from Raymond or his cellmate. There appeared to be someone in Raymond's bunk covered with a blanket, but he wasn't sure if it had moved or not.

"Raymond!" he said one more time.

This time the blankets moved, and the moan was louder. Stroe was satisfied that he was at least alive. He would check back later. He left, not seeing the string that was attached to the blankets on Raymond's bed, that ran behind the leg of the bunk and down to where Colton was pulling on them, making the blankets move.

Stroe looked at his watch and realized he needed to be at the back door. At that moment, Raymond was opening the back door and removing the metal strip. He then snapped a two-foot section off his mop handle as a weapon, should he need it, and hid the mop and bucket. He could hear a vehicle coming. He climbed into the Dumpster and covered himself with several bags of trash. The stench was nearly unbearable, and liquid that he didn't want to identify started dripping out of one of the bags, slowly covering him. He didn't dare move, though, because the truck had backed up to the back door fifteen feet away from him.

The door opened, and Officer Stroe said good morning to the milkman. They took the milk inside to the kitchen, as Raymond counted to himself. This was his chance, but he knew he couldn't go yet. Time seemed to move as if it were trapped in concrete and the stench of the Dumpster was starting to overwhelm him. He was now soaked in whatever liquid had been leaking on him. Finally, the back door opened, and they took the last load of milk inside. Raymond counted to fifteen and then jumped out of the Dumpster and ran into the milk truck.

He went all the way to the front of the truck, moved around some crates to hide behind, and settled in. it wasn't very long before the back door opened again. Officer Stroe and the milkman talked for a few minutes. Then Stroe took a look inside the truck. Raymond held his breath, hoping he was hidden well enough.

"Am I good to go?" the milkman asked, checking his watch.

"Yeah, you're good."

"Here," the milkman said, tossing him a chocolate milk. "Have one on me."

"Thanks. You have a good day," said Stroe.

"Three more stops, and I'll be having a great day."

*Three more stops. Which means I've got two stops to get out of here without getting caught.*

The truck started moving, and Raymond took his first deep breath in the last three hours.

*I did it. I'm one step away from freedom.*

He started to relax and bleed off some excess adrenaline. It was only then that two thoughts started to tug at the edges of his mind. First was how cold the truck was inside. He guessed that it was probably around thirty-eight degrees. Second was his clothes that were soaking wet from sitting in that Dumpster.

*Oh, well. A little chill is a small price to pay for getting out of hell.*

The truck kept going, with Raymond getting colder by the minute. He tried to take his mind off the cold by jogging in place and doing some jumping jacks. But after nearly knocking over a stack of milk in the pitch dark, he decided to stop. The truck slowed down, stopped, and then started backing up. Raymond tried to get back to his hiding place, but got turned around in the darkness and smacked his head on the wall, making a dull thud.

When the truck stopped and the door opened, he realized he wasn't behind the crates, but beside them. He dove out of sight before the milkman's eyes could adjust to the darkness. The milkman got a load of milk from the truck and took it to the back door of a building, hit a button, and waited. Raymond peeked out just enough to see him. The door opened, and a woman in a gray uniform stepped out to let him make his delivery.

*Great! Another prison. I would say, out of the frying pan, into the fire, but it's more like out of the fridge and into the freezer.*

He was trying to maintain a positive attitude. At least the warm air creeping into the open truck made him feel a little better. They finished the delivery, and once again the officer glanced around inside the truck. Raymond tried to make himself as small as possible. The officer seemed to take a long time looking. Suddenly, Raymond saw a flashlight shine against the back wall. He froze, not moving a muscle.

"What's this?" he heard the woman say.

Raymond gripped his piece of mop handle a little tighter. He was willing to use it if he had to. The light continued to shine in his direction.

"Oh, that's our new flavor, banana milk," the milkman said. "Would you like to try one?"

"Sure."

The milkman handled her a carton and closed the truck as they headed off to their next destination. Raymond started to shake after a few minutes. Once the door closed, the temperature plummeted. The cold soaked through is skin and into his bones, leeching away with consciousness. Lack of sleep and the mind-numbing cold conspired to lull him to sleep. He shivered and shook himself away. In this refrigerated box, sleep equaled death. Yet he was fighting a losing battle. He nodded off. He started dreaming about his nice warm bunk and warm cell and caught himself actually wishing he were there. A large bump in the road jarred him back to reality.

*I don't care what the next stop is. I need to get out of this truck.*

Fortunately, the next stop was a roadside diner. When the truck came to a stop, Raymond tried to get up but was literally frozen to the floor. He had been lying there too long in wet clothes. Try as he might, he couldn't pull himself away from the cold metal floor. He began to panic when the doors opened and the milkman started pulling milk out of the truck. There was almost not enough milk left to hide behind.

If he didn't get out right now, he knew he was busted. He pulled his pants loose, but his shirt was stuck fast. He managed to wiggle out of it, and as fast as he could, he climbed out of the truck. He made his way around to the dark side of the truck and waited with his mop handle held at the ready. When the milkman took his next load inside, Raymond dashed over to the parking lot and hid behind one of the cars. He watched as the truck pulled away.

He was free at last.

# THIRTY-THREE

Colton sat alone, cuffed to the metal chair. He examined the room with an analytical eye.

*Not very imposing in itself. But just knowing what goes on here is enough to generate fear. That, and the single light bulb for illumination.*

Emil entered the room carrying a metal chair. He sat down on it, with the back turned to Colton, and straddled it, leaning on the back to face him.

"Good morning," Emil growled.

"Good morning, Captain. How's your day going?"

"Not too good so far."

"Sorry to hear that. You look tired."

"Long night. Now, if the pleasantries are out of the way, did you help your cellmate escape?"

"Yes."

"That's it? Just, 'Yes?' No denials? No deals? Nothing?"

"I was saving myself potential pain. Eventually you would have gotten the same answer. I just saved myself the trouble of being tortured for it."

Emil shrugged.

"Understandable. So, let's have the rest. Where was he going? What was the plan if he got out?"

"I don't know."

A spark of anger kindled in Emil's eyes.

"Don't tell me that."

"It's true, Captain. I honestly don't know. That was part of the plan, so that I could have deniability, and that way you couldn't beat information out of me that I don't have."

Emil sat back and thought for a moment.

"Well played. What was the rest of it?"

"The rest of what?"

"The rest of the plan," he shouted. "I want details; names, times. I need to know where my weaknesses are."

Colton shuffled in his seat.

"That's where things get a little difficult."

"How so?"

"To tell you the entire plan would be to risk the jobs of certain officers, which means risking my life."

Emil considered this.

"So, you want protection?"

"Yes, please."

"Tell me what I want to know. Then I'll decide if you will need protection or not."

"Is that the best deal I can get?"

"That's the only deal you'll get."

"I suppose I'll have to accept that."

~

Raymond's selection of vehicles to steal wasn't very good; a station wagon that looked like it had been built from parts of a dozen other cars, and a pickup that had a fender missing and no driver's door. The station wagon had clothes in it, which made it the obvious choice. He needed to change anyway.

The wires hung down under the dash in a tangled mess. Raymond was not the best carjacker. It had been years since he had tried to hotwire a car. After four or five failed attempts, the car finally turned over. He drove about fifteen miles when he saw that the gas gauge was reading just above the E. He would need some money to make it much farther. He pulled into a driveway and, having no weapon but a two-foot piece of mop handle, he decided to pull a con instead of a straight robbery. His new clothes fit his plan perfectly. They were old rags that were four sizes too big for him. He already smelled right for the part after sitting in a Dumpster a few hours earlier.

Dawn had just broken, and he paused to look at his first daybreak as a free man.

"Pretty, ain't it?" said an older lady in a housecoat walking toward him carrying a bucket.

"Yes, ma'am," Raymond answered.

"What can I do ya for?" she asked.

"Um, I hate to bother you, I just don't know how to ask this," he said. He turned to leave.

"Now, don't go bein' like that. What's stuck in yer craw, son? Spit it out."

Raymond smiled to himself.

*Gotcha!*

"Well, I'm not in the habit of burdening others with my problems."

"Catching a gander at yer car, I'd say ya got plenty of those. Tell ol' Mama Eva what's eatin' ya, son."

"I'm trying to get across the state. I lost my job, and I heard there's work east of here."

"Aw, honey, tha's plum too bad. Lotsa folks round here been struggling too. Lucky me, I ain't been hit nearly as hard. But I ain't got no work fer ya."

"Are you sure you don't need some chores done around the farm? I just need a little money for gas. Hopefully it will get me as far as I need to go."

"I'll tell ya what, how's about I just give ya a few dollars to get you a little further down the road. Where are ya headed anyway?"

"I'm not really sure, just east."

"Well, have ya had any grub this morning?"

"No, ma'am."

"I'll fix ya up. Come on in and wash up. If ya don't mind my sayin' so, it's been a powerful long time since ya seen a washtub too, ain't it?"

Raymond feigned embarrassment.

"Yes, ma'am."

"Well, go on and wash up. I'll start cookin.'"

Raymond gladly took advantage of the chance to wash up. He took his shirt off and washed his chest and underarms. He felt like he was washing away the grime of prison. He let out a deep sigh. This was a chance to start a new life. He went back out, and the smell of a delicious breakfast cooking greeted him. Mama Eva was in the kitchen when Raymond approached.

"Just have a seat at the table, sonny. It's almost ready," she said.

He sat down at a beautiful antique table. A few minutes later, she brought out two huge plates, each loaded with steak, eggs, and biscuits. By the time she had taken her seat, Raymond had already helped himself. A forkful of steak was on it's way to his mouth when her hand reached over and slapped his.

"'Round here we say grace 'fore we eat."

Raymond was too hungry to argue. He dropped the fork onto his plate, folded his hands and closed his eyes.

She prayed, "Dear Lord, thank you for your many blessings you've given us. Thank you for providing us with food and shelter. And Lord, please watch over this young man whom you have led here. Guide him and help him along his path. Thank you, Jesus. Amen."

Raymond grabbed his fork and attacked his steak.

"Good Lord, boy, you act like you ain't had a decent meal in years."

"You could say that."

Just then, the front door opened and closed. "I'm home," yelled a man's voice. "You won't believe the night I had," he yelled as he came from the living room. "Honey, whose car is that out front?"

"We have a guest," Mama Eva said. "I never did get yer name," she said to Raymond. He started to give a phony name when the man's voice cut him off.

"Raymond Perry!"

Raymond looked up into the face of the man he had vomited on not five hours ago, and realized he had to do something quickly.

He jumped up, grabbed a steak knife, and put it to Mama Eva's throat, while dragging her to her feet and holding her in front of him like a human shield. Officer Stevens's shock wore off in a heartbeat seeing his wife held hostage. His face turned to hardened steel.

"If you harm her, I swear I'll gut you like a fish," he growled. Mama Eva was still catching up to the situation.

"Robert, why is this boy holding my steak knife to my throat?"

"He's an escaped inmate. He escaped from Larsan last night. Myself and two other officers are being held responsible for it."

"So, you mean this boy's a convict tryin' to run off without paying for his crimes?"

"Das right, Mama," Raymond answered, mocking her. "I's been a real, *real* bad boy."

He started laughing but stopped right away when the air suddenly evacuated his chest. Mama Eva had buried her elbow into Raymond's stomach, knocking the wind out of him. Officer Stevens quickly took the knife out of his hand, threw him face down on the floor, and cuffed him.

Raymond couldn't believe it. He had come so far just to trip at the finish line.

"So, what should we do with him until the police arrive?" Stevens said, with an evil grin on his face.

# THIRTY-FOUR

Raymond stewed in the patrol car while Stevens and another cop laughed at his expense. He buried his face in his hands and didn't look up until they were back at Larsan Prison.

The news of his escape and capture had reached the prison before them. When Raymond was escorted inside, all the officers looked like they were trying not to laugh at the greatest joke they had ever been told, while the inmates hung their heads, as if it were a funeral. A few days later, all those officers involved were fired, and attitudes radically reversed. The inmates acted like it was a holiday, while the officers skulked around with rage in their eyes, daring any inmate to laugh to their face.

Raymond sat in the dark RHU cell, utterly alone. He couldn't sleep; his coughing fits kept him awake. His ride in the freezer truck landed him a low-grade case of pneumonia, but medical refused to see him. He was left to suffer through it.

His only human contact was three times a day when an officer shoved a tray through his cell door. He made a mental note to never again complain about prison food.

The nights here were dark. The only light that filtered into his cell came from a bare bulb, 15 feet down the hall, and it was only bright enough to allow the guards to patrol the block. It provided little comfort.

It was unnervingly quiet at night, although the prison itself made noises - some real, some imagined; creaks and groans from pipes; every once in a while a rattle or bang of a cell door when someone came or left.

*"You can always tell whether someone is coming or going,"* Raymond mused. *"They're loud when they come in, deathly silent when they leave."*

Raymond sank into an abyss of depression. Just when he thought he couldn't sink any lower, the cell door opened ... and in walked Captain Sorn.

*Express elevator goin' down!*

The captain walked over to his bunk and sat beside him. Raymond cringed waiting for the beating to begin. Sorn just slapped his knee.

"Don't worry, kid, I'm not gonna hurt you," Emil said.

Raymond eyed him suspiciously.

"You're an inmate. Inmates try to escape. Our job as officers is to stop them."

His countenance changed in a heartbeat, and his voice was like gravel crunching under the weight of an 18-wheeler"

"Three of my officers failed to do that job. And I have you to thank for that."

Raymond backed away from him.

"Three of my officers who have ruined their careers, who won't be able to provide for their families, who brought shame to this institution."

Emil's speech slowed. You could feel the pressure in the air like the onset of an impending thunderstorm.

"Three officers who could be facing criminal charges. All because you were being selfish. All because you didn't feel like paying for your crimes," he whispered.

Emil rose to his feet. His eyes were unfocused as though he wasn't in the room. He towered over Raymond, fists clenched, face red, looking as though he were a volcano about to erupt. What stopped him, Raymond wasn't sure. But for a moment he stood still looking like a robot that had to pause and reboot. And just like that, he came to his senses.

"It's not your fault, though," Emil smiled. "Nothing is *ever* the fault of *any* inmate, right? *Everyone* here is innocent, right? Your victims had it coming, right?"

Emil turned toward the cell door, then stopped.

"Besides, we all have something to laugh about now. Maybe we could get you in one of those books about world's most stupid inmates. I mean, of all the houses to stop at."

He started laughing. It wasn't a pleasant sound. It was more like the evil chuckle of a predator toying with its prey. As the door slammed shut, Raymond started thinking about how to tie slipknots into his sheets.

# THIRTY-FIVE

Warden Alton Randall Bennington III. That's what the nameplate on his desk proclaimed.

The nameplate was oversized - perhaps to compensate for its owner's physical shortcomings - and quite impressive. It personified Alton in more ways than he realized.

Although he boasted a puffed-up resume and appeared politically impressive, in truth he was an oversized paperweight, a figurehead, a puppet ruler whose primary claim to fame came from taking credit for the hard work of others.

He sometimes felt that he was taking advantage of Captain Sorn. He got to go to all the political functions, benefits, and dinners. He extolled the virtues of a strong corrections system, while building his own political status. It was the perfect situation for him.

Yet something wasn't sitting quite right, like an itch between his shoulder blades that he couldn't quite reach. 'Sorn.' The name wormed its way into his brain. He tried to shove it away, but it niggled its way back, burrowed deep, and refused to be dislodged.

Sorn had been a good and loyal employee, handling all the day-to-day crap so Bennington didn't have to exert himself. Oh, there had been the occasion complaint, the hints of improprieties and crossing the line; but that was just part of Corrections. Bennington had developed a system for dealing with such reports – he placed them in a file, shoved the file in the lower drawer of his desk, locked the drawer and never looked at the file again ... until the next report. Lately the reports were coming hard and fast. Sorn's file was getting fat.

He decided to delve into this problem, to see if it was as serious as people made it out to be. He looked at the file drawer as if it were the harbinger of bad news. Reluctantly, he unlocked it and pulled out Emil's file that had grown by leaps and bounds. He opened the file and read the most recent report.

"Raymond Perry," he mused, something about the name tickling his memory. "Still in RHU. Perhaps I should pay a visit to Mr. Perry."

~

Warden Alton Randall Bennington III stormed back into his office, slammed the door behind him and locked it. He paced. He fumed. He jerked open the bottom drawer of his filing cabinet that harbored the good stuff, and pulled out a dusty, never opened bottle of 30-year-old Château de Montifaud cognac, took a deep breath and cracked the seal.

"I was saving you for a special occasion," he said aloud, "but I think this takes precedence." He called to the lieutenant on shift and had Raymond moved back to his old cell.

The next day, Emil slammed both fists down on the warden's desk and screamed at the man sitting on the other side.

"Who do you think you are putting my inmate back in general population?"

"He's been in RHU long enough."

"You don't get to make that decision."

"I'm the warden; I run this place!"

"I run this place. I have for years! You go to your little meetings and conferences while I keep the place running smooth, and you looking good. So just shut your mouth, sign the checks, and we'll be just fine." Emil leaned in and lowered his voice to a menacing growl. "Remember, Alton, if I go down, I'm taking you with me."

Sorn turned and left without another word. Bennington was shaken, even trembling. He pulled out the half empty bottle of cognac and poured himself another large glass.

*How did it come to this? How could I have been so blind?*

He knew the answer, of course, but admitting that he had let someone take advantage of him was a difficult pill to swallow. He weighed his options.

*One, I turn a blind eye and keep enjoying the perks while letting a monster roam loose. Two, I fight, try to make a difference. Or three, I give up and slink away with my tail between my legs.*

He knew what had to be done. He just didn't feel like ending his career.

Two days later, Emil was called to the warden's office. He was in the middle of filling brown boxes with his personal possessions.

"So, you're giving up, are you?" he said to Alton, with an arrogant smirk. "That's good; you'll have more time to spend on your political career."

The veiled threat was not lost on the warden, as he continued packing.

"Do you have anything for me before you go?" Emil asked.

"Like what?"

## CHAPTER 35

"Like the file you keep on me. Don't think I don't know about it."

Alton tried to keep a guilty look off his face.

"And if such a file existed, why should I give it to you?"

Emil stepped closer. "Because you're not out of this prison yet, and all kinds of bad things happen to people in a prison. Most times they don't see it coming."

Alton looked up at the sheer size of the man, and then he looked into his eyes.

*I never noticed the coldness there.* He mused. *I never saw the monster. Was he always like this?*

He reached into the file drawer and pulled out a large file.

"I'm not sure I should ... " he started, but Emil snatched it out of his hands. He opened it and looked through it. It was all there. Every write-up from his file, testimonies, and interviews implicating him in several illegal activities, including one-on-ones. He smiled and turned to leave but then stopped.

"Enjoy your retirement. I hope the next warden has a little more spirit."

After he left, the warden said, "I hope so too."

# THIRTY-SIX

Eighty-Seven miles from Larsan prison stood the maximum-security prison at Crestman. It was a modern, top of the line, facility, but it still had problems.

Lieutenant Teph shouted through the door for the second time, "Get back over to the cell door and cuff up."

Inmate Cyril Chatham stayed where he was, kneeling in the corner, with his hands covering his face. His body was lurching, as though he was praying while sobbing into his hands. The lieutenant used pepper spray on Chatham a second time. He sprayed the back wall hoping that some splatter might hit him in the face. He waited for a few moments to let the spray take effect and disable Chatham. He gave the order again, sprayed more, and then waited.

The inmate continued kneeling and covering his face. Five officers in helmets and body armor stood behind the lieutenant awaiting his command. He sprayed one more time, waited thirty seconds, and then gave the order for the team to secure the inmate. As soon as the door opened, everything changed.

Inmate Chatham jumped up, wheeled around, and started laughing. He had baby powder all over his face, making him look like a deranged ghost. The lead officer ran in with a riot shield trying to pin the inmate against the wall. He didn't notice how shiny the floor was.

Chatham had dumped shampoo all over it an hour earlier, anticipating this moment. The officer slipped and went headfirst into the wall, knocking him unconscious and out of the fight. Chatham used this to his advantage, standing on top of the downed officer for traction. The second officer tried to secure him with handcuffs. He managed to get one cuff on his wrist, and tried to pull his arm into a submission hold. However, Chatham had anticipated this and had a dozen pencils wrapped around his wrists under his sweatshirt.

He slipped out of the cuff, turned it around, and cuffed the officer. Lieutenant Teph realized it had been a setup, and Chatham was playing possum to draw them into his cell. Things were quickly turning in Chatham's favor. Teph had to act quickly. He was not in body armor, but he charged into the cell with the last three officers on the team.

He sprayed OC in Chatham's face as he came. Chatham merely wiped it off of the baby powder and felt no effects. Teph realized this would have to be done the hard way. The officer in front of Teph stumbled over the unconscious bodies, and then he received the toe of Chatham's boot right under his chin, underneath the protection of the helmet. The kick was worthy of a pro football player. One more officer down.

The remaining officers, and Teph, tackled Chatham and tried to get leg restraints on him. He kicked Teph off, but Teph recovered, buried his knee into Chatham's groin, and then placed leg restraints on him while he was doubled over in pain. They rolled him over, and Teph kneeled on Chatham's neck while the officers cuffed him. Chatham got up and spat in Teph's face. Teph wiped it off and said,

"Take him to RHU."

As they were taking him out of the cell, the officers *accidentally* smashed Chatham's head into the cell wall.

"No!" Teph shouted at the officers. "He has been secured. Take him to RHU, without any accidents."

The officers complied. Once he was in his cell, the nurse came and examined his injuries without incident. Afterward, she returned to the infirmary and examined the officers on the extraction team. As the nurse was finishing up with Lt. Teph, he was called to the warden's office.

~

"You wanted to see me, sir?" Teph asked.

"Yes, come in, have a seat," Warden Stanton said. "I wanted to talk to you about your performance."

Teph was somewhat abashed.

"I take full responsibility for the team's actions, sir. Chatham was well prepared for us. I know that's no excuse, but we did secure him, with minimal damage. If any discipline needs to be handed down, I should be the first to receive it."

Stanton stopped him.

"I know what happened. It wasn't your fault or your team's fault. He set you up with an ambush. As far as I'm concerned, you did what needed to be done."

Teph relaxed a bit.

"Why did you call me here then, sir?"

"Are you happy working here at Crestman Prison?"

"Yes, sir."

"Have you thought about anywhere else?"

"Not really, sir."

"Do you have any higher aspirations?"

"Such as?"

"Such as taking my job," the warden said.

"Sir, I would never try anything against you. You taught

me all I know about being a lieutenant."

"Calm down, Michael. I didn't mean anything subversive or undermining. I know you better than that. I simply meant have you ever thought about being a warden?"

"I'm sorry, sir, I thought you meant—"

"No. I trust you implicitly to have the best interests of everyone in mind and to perform your duties with the utmost integrity." A look of concern passed the warden's face. "That's why I almost hate to speak to you about this. A warden friend of mine is having trouble at his prison. It's more than he can handle, and he called me for help."

"I'm flattered that you would think of me, sir."

"You won't be when I tell you where it is."

Teph hesitated.

"Oh no, not ... "

"Yep, Larsan."

Teph's face fell, but only for an instant. Then he said, "If you think I can help, I trust you, sir, and I will do my best to be a good lieutenant at Larsan."

"That's great, but I'm not asking you to be a lieutenant. I'm asking you to be warden."

Teph's mouth dropped open.

"Sir, I don't know what to say."

"First of all, you can say, 'yes.'"

"Yes. Of course, yes."

"Good. Second, you can stop acting like I've done you a great favor. Larsan is the worst prison in the state. You'll have a lot of work to do."

"I understand, sir. I'll do my best."

"I know you will; that's why I recommended you. Now, I will give you one piece of advice that I have always believed in: give the illusion of knowledge. Even if you're not sure about something, never let that be seen. Not by your staff, officers, and especially not by the inmates.

Taking suggestions is fine, but in the end, you be the one to say, 'This is what we're going to do.' If you make a mistake, do your best to fix it, but always show strength, because others will draw strength from you. I know this is a lot to ask. Do you think you can handle it?"

"Yes, sir."

# THIRTY-SEVEN

The secretary was checking her e-mails when the phone rang.

"Larsan State Prison, how may I help you?" she answered.

"Patrice, it's Emil."

"Good morning, Captain. I thought you had today off."

"So did I, until I found out that we are about to have a visitor."

"Really? I don't see anything on my schedule."

"Trust me, it's happening. When he gets there just stall him."

"How will I know who he is?"

"He's about my size, and his name is Michael Teph."

"Yes, sir, consider him stalled."

Michael Teph walked through the door half an hour later.

"May I help you?" Patrice said.

"I'm looking for Captain Sorn."

"May I ask your name?"

"Michael Teph. I'm the new warden."

"Oh, well, it's nice to meet you. If you have a seat, I'll call him."

"Why don't you just show me where my new office is and I can wait for him there?"

"I'm not sure if the captain wants ..."

"What did you say your name was?"

"Umm ... Patrice."

"Well, Patrice, why don't you show me to my office or you can sit in the unemployment line."

"Yes, sir."

~

An hour later there was a knock on Warden Teph's door.

"Come in," he said.

Emil strode through the door trying to look as imposing as possible. The warden was looking through papers and didn't bother to look up.

"Can I help you?"

"I'm Captain Sorn."

Teph looked up from his papers, eyed Emil up and down, then said, "Captain Sorn. Please have a seat."

"Yes, sir."

"I wanted to familiarize myself with the staff here. So, tell me, Captain, what are your goals for this prison, and how do you think we can accomplish them?"

"Well, sir, my goals are the safety of my people, keeping inmates in line, and making sure that every inmate gets what is coming to him. Those goals can be accomplished by letting me do my job, my way."

"I see. So, you see no improvement needed here?"

"None."

"Thank you for your time."

Sorn recognized the dismissal, rose, and left.

Warden Teph stared at the door.

*This is going to be a challenge.*

~

Colton startled awake. He looked up to see four faces obscured by riot helmets and feared for his life. He wondered at the identity of the men, but a half-decent guess could tell who they were. Colton looked into the eyes of the tallest of the four and mentally exchanged a silent question.

*I thought we had a deal?*

The man gave him a knowing look and turned away as the team quietly surrounded the bunk. Colton closed his eyes and braced for the inevitable, but all he heard were muffled shouts. He opened his eyes to see Raymond being carried out of the cell, bound and gagged with a bag over his head. The tallest team member closed the cell door and looked at Colton again before catching up with the team.

Colton leaned back in his bunk feeling relieved. Then guilt crept up on him and overwhelmed him. He covered his eyes with a dry washcloth that slowly became wet, as he thought of what Raymond was about to go through.

When they took the bag off Raymond's head, he was cuffed to the little metal chair again. Captain Sorn was standing directly in front of him tapping his baton into his palm.

"Why am I here, sir?" Raymond asked.

His answer was a baton across the jaw, nearly breaking it.

"You're here because I brought you here. I wanted to have a little chat, and lying to me would be most unwise. What did you tell the warden?"

"About what, sir?"

"About me, about the program, about anything."

"Nothing, sir."

"I don't believe you." The baton whistled through the

air, impacting with Raymond's kneecap, shattering it. Raymond screamed in pain.

"I ... didn't ... tell ... him ... anything," he said through gritted teeth.

Sorn looked dubious.

"I thought you'd lie to me, so I invited a few of your old buddies here to talk to you."

Out of the shadows came three men. Raymond recognized two immediately. The third was no mystery, considering the other two. They were former officers Okrie, Stroe, and Stevens. They stood around him, each carrying a baton. Raymond said nothing, and neither did they. There was no need; they would do all their talking with their batons.

"These officers," Sorn said. "Scratch that ... these former officers wish to share a few complaints with you over the careers you stole from them."

Then he struck a blow to Raymond's head with his baton. Raymond nearly blacked out, not even feeling the next several blows that rained down on him. He knew better than to struggle. He just tried to curl up as much as possible and take it. His body was withstanding the punishment until he felt the first vertebra crack. He lurched forward and tried to cry out. But a baton smashed into his mouth, knocking out several teeth.

Raymond tried again and again to plead for them to stop, but every time he tried, they grew more enraged. His life began to flash one scene at a time every time the baton pummeled him.

*Crack,* he was born.

*Crack,* at nine his mother left.

*Crack,* at eleven he stole his first candy bar.

*Crack,* at twelve he had his first trip to juvenile hall.

*Crack,* at seventeen his father died.

*Crack,* at twenty he committed his first armed robbery.

It finally sunk in that he had truly wasted his life, and for the first time, he felt remorse. But it was too late. Raymond's life ended at thirty-one years, four months, and twenty-three days, in Larsan State Prison.

The officers were in such a bloodlust rage that they continued raining blows on the corpse. Only when they realized that it had been some time since Raymond had reacted to the assault did they finally stop. They backed away in unison, each covered in blood, and stared at the lump of meat in the chair that didn't even resemble a human body anymore.

Stevens dropped his baton, fell to his knees, and clutched his chest. The other three grabbed him and took him to the hospital.

The hospital staff asked lots of questions. Emil answered them all, saying that they were slaughtering a pig when Stevens collapsed. The doctor on duty was not convinced. He called a friend who happened to be a deputy sheriff and explained the situation.

"Really? Covered in blood?" he asked.

"Yes. Would you mind coming over and checking it out?"

"I'll be right there."

# THIRTY-EIGHT

Warden Teph was sitting in his apartment watching *The Shawshank Redemption*. Being a bachelor, he had every excuse to let the place get messy, yet the apartment was meticulously clean, if sparsely decorated. He simply refused to let things go. If there was a job to do, he took care of it right away. That was just his personality.

His first week as the new warden had been an interesting one. He hadn't gotten the chance to get out on the floor much. The captain kept him buried in paperwork that he said was urgent. However, Teph was beginning to suspect that Emil didn't want him to even see the rest of the prison. He took time to scrutinize the personnel files of all the prison employees, paying particular interest to the officers who had been recently fired. He studied the names and pictures of each one involved, including Raymond Perry. He tried to interview Raymond two days ago, but he just wasn't talking. It seemed odd to have such a sense of fear instilled in a hardened inmate. This made him even more curious about the case.

His attention was drawn back to the here and now by the ending of the movie. He got up, stretched, and headed for the bedroom when the phone rang.

"Hello?"

"Is this Warden Teph?"

"Yes. Who is this?"

"This is Deputy Collins with the Larsan Sherriff's Department."

"What can I do for you, Deputy?" Teph said, stifling a yawn.

"I'm down here at the hospital. I got a report of three men bringing in another man complaining of chest pains."

"OK, that sounds pretty standard, not really worthy of a report."

"I would agree, except all four men were covered in blood."

"That would warrant investigating. Forgive me, Deputy, but what exactly does this have to do with me?"

"I was getting to that. The doctor said one of the men was wearing a Larsan State Prison uniform."

Teph's blood turned to ice.

"Are you sure?"

"The doctor is sure."

"Can I speak with him?"

"He just went off duty."

"Can you get me his phone number?"

Silence on the other end.

"I'm not sure ... " Collins said slowly. "I don't think that would be a good idea while I'm investigating this incident."

Teph breathed a deep, calming breath.

"Look, I'm going to need to launch an investigation of my own, and you're giving me nothing to work with here. I have nearly four hundred staff members, plus it's possible that one of my twelve hundred inmates could've stolen an officer's uniform. I'm talking about the security of my prison and your town."

Collins hesitated. "I can give you the name of the patient."

~

Stevens slowly opened his eyes. The pain medication had made him groggy. He remembered a dream about being tied down and people in blue gowns cutting him open. He tried to orient himself by looking around the room. It was bright, but had no decoration. A curtain hung in the middle of the room. It smelled like disinfectant, and the constant beeping of machines distracted him. His eyes fell on a large man sitting in the chair beside his bed. He flinched involuntarily.

"Good morning, Mr. Stevens," Warden Teph said. "You gave the doctors a bit of a scare. Not everybody survives a triple bypass."

"What do you want?" he croaked.

"Not much," he said, leaning back in his seat. "Just a few words and one straight answer."

"I can give you as many words as you want. Most of them have four letters."

"That wasn't very polite."

"How polite am I supposed to be to the man who took my job?" he rasped.

"No, Raymond Perry took your job. Or more like, you gave it to him. He's the one you should've thanked, or is that what you were doing in my prison, thanking him personally?"

Stevens looked away.

"That's what I thought. You know, I've changed my mind. You've already given me my answer. I only need two words from you. I can guess that Mr. Okrie and Mr. Stroe were two of the people with you. I only need the name of the last person."

Stevens turned back toward Warden Teph and smiled.

"You have no idea who you're dealing with."

"Thank you for that cliché, but yes, I do. Right now I'm

dealing with you," Teph said, standing and towering over Stevens. "And you are dealing with murder charges. Is your anonymous friend placed high enough to get you out of that?"

"You can't prove anything."

"Please," Teph said. "I have a dead inmate, and I have Okrie and Stroe. Let's see if they are as devoted to keeping the mystery man's identity secret. I have also kept this a local investigation, for now. All I need to do is pick up the phone and it becomes national news."

"You can't. What about my family?"

"That's up to you."

Stevens pondered his options.

"I can't," he said quietly. "He'll kill me."

Teph leaned in until he was an inch away from Stevens's face.

"Who says I won't?"

Stevens looked at him in shock.

Teph turned his attention to the many machines that were plugged into the wall attached to Stevens by myriad wires and tubes.

"I wonder what this does," Teph said, as he pulled a plug out of its wall socket.

"What are you doing?"

"Nothing," he said, with mock innocence while pulling out another cord.

Stevens watched in horror as lights on the machine faded.

"Stop!" Stevens screamed.

"I don't know what you're talking about," Teph replied.

"Nicoles! His name is Nicoles!"

"How long has he been an officer at the prison?"

"I don't know. Nobody is supposed to know anybody else. We aren't even part of the group. Nicoles called us."

"Why?"

"Plug my cord back in, please."

"After you tell me what you know."

"I could die!"

"Then you'd better talk fast."

He nervously looked at the dangling plug.

"It's a shadow justice group led by one man—Nicoles. He calls a victim of an inmate housed in Larsan that he's been having trouble with and invites them to "exercise true justice."

"And what does that mean?"

"He has the victim come in after hours and gives them a pep talk about now being the time to avenge themselves for the injustice that's been done to them. And then they walk in the room, torture their tormentor, and Nicoles is clean. He gets his troublemakers taken care of without getting his hands dirty."

"I told you what you wanted, now plug my machine back in!"

Teph smiled as he turned and walked away.

"Hey!"

Teph stopped. "Don't worry, these machines run on batteries. They were fully charged. Thanks for the info, though."

Stevens watched through a mask of anger as Teph walked out the door. He reached for the phone and began to dial.

"Yes?"

"He fell for it."

"Good."

"Now, what about my hospital bills? I don't have insurance anymore."

"Don't worry, we'll take care of you," the man said. Then he hung up the phone.

Something about the way he said it made Stevens nervous.

# THIRTY-NINE

Teph drove back to the prison and searched through all the personnel files looking for an officer named Nicoles. His frustration grew the longer the search went. He checked every file he could find, when Captain Sorn knocked on his door.

"Come in!" Teph said, a little more gruffly than he'd intended.

"You called for me, sir?" Sorn asked, looking at the stacks of files littering the office.

Teph looked up with bleary eyes.

"I'm trying to find someone."

"I know a lot of someone's, could you be more specific?"

"Nicoles."

Sorn clucked his tongue and shook his head.

"If you're looking for Nicoles, you've got your hands full," Sorn said.

"So, you know him?"

"I know *of* him. No one *knows* him. He's like an urban legend, a ghost that disappears as soon as you look his way."

"So, he's just fiction then?"

"On the contrary. He's real, but no one has ever caught him."

"Why not?"

"Because he's more than one person."

"How is that possible?"

"I've spent years investigating one-on-ones. Every time I get close to the truth, it evaporates. I've had the camera in room 114 fixed several times. It breaks mysteriously every time there's an incident. I believe there is a shadow group within the prison that knows the inner workings and disappears when they feel someone is on to them."

"So, it's impossible to catch them."

"No, I wouldn't say that. I've come close several times. The real problem is anytime someone gets in trouble, they blame Nicoles. It's tough to find someone who's invisible."

"So how do we make the invisible visible?"

"By kicking up a whole lot of dirt."

Teph thought quietly for a moment.

"Captain Sorn," he said. "I am hereby authorizing you to use whatever personnel and materials necessary to track down and expose this group."

"I'll do my best, sir," Sorn said on his way out the door.

Emil Sorn had a difficult time keeping his car on the road on his way home—he was laughing so hard.

~

The shakedown that followed was one of the largest the facility had ever seen and the toughest. Inmates left and right were going to RHU for breaking rules that hadn't been enforced in years. RHU filled up overnight. Angry inmates complained and threatened to sue. The captain responded to each one with the same message: Talk to the warden.

The warden was inundated with requests and grievances. To his credit, the warden backed the officers in every inmate complaint. He answered them saying that these rules had been in place for a long time, and choosing to enforce them was perfectly legal. The officers were skeptical at first, but once things started improving, they realized that the warden really cared. They were impressed with the support and backing they got from the warden. He even went a step farther in going to each shift briefing and commending the officers for a job well done. He started spending more time on the floor talking to officers about problems with the facility and what could be done to solve them.

At first Emil was secretly amused by the whole thing, but then a nagging thought burrowed into his brain. What if the officers actually started believing in Teph? He might find a weak link. Not only had he failed to make the warden look bad, but now some of Emil's officers were starting to buy into Teph. One day the warden was on the floor touring when he went into central control. He exchanged idle chitchat with the officer when he noticed a dark image on one of the monitors.

"What's wrong here?" he asked the officer, who suddenly looked nervous.

"Um ... that camera's broken, sir."

"What room is that?"

"Room 114, sir. It's a large multipurpose room."

"Well, get maintenance on that."

"Yes, sir."

Teph started to leave when the officer spoke up.

"Sir, can I ask you a question?"

"Ask away."

"Do you really care about what goes on here?"

"Does it look like I care?"

"Yes, sir, it really does. That's why I asked the question."

The warden grinned.

"If I didn't care, I wouldn't be here."

"Yes, sir."

"What's your name?"

"Neil Redland, sir."

The warden took out a little notebook and wrote in it. Then he smiled and said, "Keep up the good work."

He returned to his office, looked up Redland's file and found it to be impeccable. He was an off-the-radar type. Never got into trouble, was a good officer, came in and did his job, and then went home to his family. A totally boring file, just the way Teph liked it. He filed the name in the back of his mind and went about his routine. A week later he was on the floor, went into central, and noticed the camera was still not fixed.

"Has maintenance been informed about this?" the warden said.

"I'm not sure, sir. I'd have to check," the officer replied.

He nodded and started to leave, pausing for a moment.

"Is officer Redland working a different post today?" Teph asked.

The officer squirmed a little.

"He doesn't work day shift anymore."

"Since when?"

"Five days ago, sir. He was transferred to evening shift."

"Transferred by whom?"

"The captain, sir."

The warden stayed late that day. He went to central about an hour after shift change. Redland stiffened as soon as the warden walked in.

"How are you?" Teph asked.

"Just fine, sir," he said briskly.

"Got moved I see."

"Yes, sir."

"How do you like it?"

Redland didn't answer.

"Were you asked to come here, or ordered to?"

"I do my job, sir. Is there anything else? I'm rather busy," Redland said.

"No, officer, there's nothing else. You have a good shift tonight."

"Thank you, sir."

The warden started to leave.

"Excuse me, sir. You dropped this."

Redland handed him a small slip of paper and shot him a knowing look.

"Thank you, officer."

He quickly put it in his pocket and left. It wasn't until he was in his car halfway home that he opened it.

It said "555-2938 after 12:30 a.m." That was all.

Teph sat in his chair, nursing a scotch and water while an obnoxious infomercial played on the television. He drummed his fingers on the arm of the chair, checking his watch every couple of minutes, cursing the second hand for dawdling. *Will 12:30 never get here?*

Finally, he dialed the number. It rang four times and went to voice mail. Not feeling like it would be the wisest thing to leave a message, he hung up and tried again in a half hour. Again, no answer.

Half the night, he repeated this process, each time getting more frustrated. After five o'clock, he stopped trying and went to sleep.

The next day, the morning report had a brief note in it that an officer had been injured during a cell extraction. The captain had requested this officer specifically, and he was the only one hurt. He read the name Neil Redland and knew what had happened. Teph immediately called Redland's wife to check on him. He was in a coma from multiple strikes to the head. The warden apologized to her and asked if there was anything she needed.

"Justice," was all she said, and then she hung up the phone.

# FORTY

Teph sat dejected in his office. Across from him, trying to keep his composure, sat Captain Sorn.

"What happened?" Teph asked.

"As close as I can tell, one of the members of the team was in with Nicoles."

"But why Redland?"

"Maybe they thought he was a threat. He had requested a move to second shift, so I put him on the extraction team so he could get a feel for how they run their team. Never in a million years did I think it would turn out like this."

"You shouldn't blame yourself, Captain. Sometimes things just go bad. Maybe when we review the tape we can find something out."

"The tape?" Emil said, starting to sweat.

"Yes, the videotape of the incident."

"Oh yes ... I forgot to bring it."

"Well, go get it," Teph said. "I've got some time."

"Yes, sir," Emil said, heading to his office. He got a blank tape out of his desk drawer and then went to RHU.

The end of the hall, last cell, farthest away from the officer's station was where they housed the worst of the worst. Inmate Hague went into that cell just yesterday.

Emil peered into the filthy, darkened cell.

"Nice digs," he said.

A mountainous shadow stirred in the corner.

"What the hell do you want?" the shadow asked, in a voice that sounded like a gravel truck.

"I came to check on you, to see how you are."

"Humph ... unlikely," the mass said, lumbering toward the cell door. "I took care of your snitch. Now what else do you want?"

"I brought you a present," Emil said.

Hague was intrigued. He looked toward the door and saw Sorn holding a small videotape.

"OK, I'm guessing this isn't a porno of you and your sweet ex-wife."

"No. It's the extraction recording of you assaulting Officer Redland."

Hague looked at the tape and licked his lips.

"So, what do I have to do?"

"Take it and destroy it."

He walked over and picked up the tape.

"That's it?" Hague said. "What's the catch?"

"The catch is we have to make it look good," Emil said to Hague. He grabbed his radio. "All available officers to RHU!"

Hague glared at Emil with rage in his eyes.

"You set me up!"

Officers arrived, and Hague's cell door was opened. A melee ensued as five officers tried to subdue Hague, but he threw them off one by one. Emil charged and tackled Hague into a wall, but a nasty blow to the back left Emil lying on the floor as Hague fought off the other officers. When Emil recovered, he grabbed Hague from behind in a headlock. The other officers, seeing the inmate was distracted, tried to rush him and push him to the floor. As they did, he fell sideways, hitting his head on the wall. Emil felt the snap and Hague's body go limp.

"Medical to RHU, ASAP," Emil said into his radio.

The nurse arrived in two minutes, and after a quick exam, the officers carried Hague to the infirmary. Emil was left alone. He looked around the demolished cell and noticed the videotape laying on the floor, miraculously untouched. Emil stomped on the tape over and over until it was in pieces.

"Captain Sorn, report to the warden's office," came a call over the radio.

Emil stumbled into the warden's office and collapsed into a chair. Warden Teph stared in shock at the bruised and disheveled captain who had left his office in immaculate condition not twenty minutes before.

"What happened to you?" Teph asked.

"I miscalculated. I got the tape like you asked but thought I could get some information out of inmate Hague if I showed him that I had the video as a trump card."

"I'm thinking that didn't turn out so well."

"Not so much, no. He grabbed the tape from me. That's when I called the officers so we could get it back. Unfortunately, it got destroyed in the fight."

Sorn set a small mound of shattered plastic in the middle of Warden Teph's desk.

"Well, that's not the only unfortunate thing that's happened in the last twenty minutes," Teph said. "Hague is dead."

"Dead?" Emil said, shock etched his face.

"Yes, apparently a broken neck."

Emil stared blankly at the warden.

"I had him in a headlock, when I felt him go limp. I thought he had passed out."

"You and your officers need to write me reports on this incident."

"Yes, sir," Emil said, slowly rising to leave.

"And, Captain; cover your bases."

"Yes, sir."

Emil went into his office, locked the door, and closed the blinds. Sitting behind his desk, a slow grin crept across his face.

"I'd like to thank the Academy ..." he said, before bursting into laughter.

# FORTY-ONE

Y ou requested to see me?" Emil said.

"Yes sir, Captain Sorn. I wanted to apologize for my previous actions, sir," Harley said loud enough for the other inmates to hear. "You were right, and I promise I won't give you any more problems, sir."

Emil eyed him suspiciously but merely said, "Good," and turned to walk away.

"Hold on a minute," Harley said.

Emil turned back and glared at him. Harley quickly added, "Please."

"What do you really want?" Emil snarled.

"OK," Harley said so that only Emil could hear. "I put on that little show to give you back the respect that I took from you with the inmates."

Emil relaxed just a little.

"That's appreciated," he said quietly.

"I wanted to talk to you, not inmate to captain, but Harley to Emil."

"OK."

"When you and I were kids," Harley started, "you beat me into submission and told me I needed counseling. I realized you were right, and it changed my life. Now as an adult, you've beat me into submission again, only now it's my turn to tell you that ... you need counseling."

"For what?" Emil demanded.

"Don't you see the hate and rage that's consuming you?"

"This conversation is over!"

"You have to get this under control before someone else gets killed."

Emil lunged at Harley, grabbed him by the throat, and pinned him to the wall, with a loud thud.

Harley grunted in pain.

"I will not be lectured by some stinking inmate!" Emil screamed.

Harley stared into Emil's eyes. There was no trace of the good person he used to call friend.

"I'm sorry I wasted your time," Harley croaked. Defeat and sadness overwhelmed the physical pain.

Emil released him, then pulled out his notepad and jotted down Harley's name.

"Sleep well," Emil growled. "You and I have an appointment tomorrow."

Harley rubbed his neck and whispered a silent prayer.

**The Next Day...11:00 a.m.**

Harley sweated out the morning knowing that Emil wouldn't just forget it or let it slide. He knew that another beating was just around the corner. As if on cue, two guards showed up and told him to pack his stuff.

*This is new. Maybe they'll take my things straight to the infirm, to save time.*

He packed, and they escorted him down the hall. He briefly entertained the thought of escape but knew it would only be worse when they caught him. He was so lost in thought that he didn't realize they weren't going to room 114. They turned down another hallway and ended up in a room with a cage. A bored-looking guard handed him a box with his name on it, pointed to an open door and said, "Change."

Harley started putting on his street clothes.

*What kind of game is this? Is he going to pretend I'm escaping so he can shoot me?*

Harley's anxiety rose by the minute. He came back out of the room and was met by another officer. He took Harley out a different door, which led outside to a fenced-in tunnel. The officer stopped at the door. Harley turned back toward him.

"Am I supposed to wait for you?"

"No, you're supposed to walk!"

He pointed down the tunnel, and Harley started walking. When he got to the end, the gates opened for him. He walked slowly to the other side of the gate, looking at the guard tower. None of them seemed too concerned about him. They were watching him but had their rifles across their chests, instead of pointing them at him.

"Hey! You! What are you doing?" yelled a man from the direction of the parking lot. Harley jumped and whipped around to see a tall, thin man in his mid-forties wearing jeans and a T-shirt covered by a sport jacket. He was leaning against an unmarked police car, smiling. Harley let out a sigh of relief and walked over to him.

"Give me a heart attack, why don't you?" Harley said.

Jack looked over his bruised arms and broken nose.

"It looks like someone hasn't been playing nice with the other children."

"You have no idea," Harley said as he collapsed into the passenger seat of the police car. Jack hopped behind the wheel.

"Well, did you find what you were looking for?"

"Unfortunately," Harley said.

**Twelve Hours Later**

"Warden Teph, there's a call for you on line one."

"Thank you, Patrice," he told his secretary. "Hello?"

"Warden, this is Officer Richardson of the Larsan State Police. I wonder if I might have a little bit of your time."

"Absolutely. I want good relations with local law enforcement. You can set up a time with my secretary…"

"Actually, sir, I'd like to meet outside the prison, if that's all right with you."

"I'm rather busy; meeting here would help me out."

"I can't. Some of your officers might recognize me, and I'd like to avoid that."

"OK, where would you like to meet?"

"There's a small café about twenty miles south of the prison called Mom's Kitchen. Do you know it?"

"Yes, I've been there."

"Good, can you meet me in an hour?"

"Um … " Teph said, flipping through his schedule.

"I guarantee you need to see what I'm going to show you."

"OK, I'll be there."

"Thank you."

Fifty-eight minutes later, they were both seated at a booth. Officer Richardson slid a manila folder to Warden Teph.

"Read that, and tell me what you think."

A young woman who appeared barely out of her teens approached the table as Teph scanned through the file. She had black fingernails, and hair that couldn't decide if it was blue or purple. Each of her ears was full of piercings as well as her lips. Harley wasn't sure, but it almost looked like she had horns beginning to grow on her forehead too. Both men stopped and stared at her wondering what she could possibly want with them.

"What can I get for you fellas?" she said, pulling out an order pad.

"Just coffee for me," Teph answered, then went back to his reading.

"I'll take the big breakfast, plus a steak, medium-well, and an extra plate of bacon," Harley said.

"Sure thing," she said, winking at Harley.

"Hasn't anyone been feeding you for a while?" Teph said.

"Your prison isn't exactly known for good cooking or second helpings."

"What do you mean?"

"Keep reading, it's all in there."

Teph read as Harley's food came. His eyes got wider with each successive page.

"This can't be."

"Unfortunately, it is. I witnessed it with my own eyes."

"What?"

Richardson looked a little embarrassed.

"I was recently a guest in your prison," he said. "I was sent in undercover, to investigate reports of corruption."

Teph sat back in his seat and eyed Richardson.

"So, am I under investigation?"

"Everyone was under investigation, but you were cleared. As was most of your staff," Richardson said. "It was just a few individuals ... one in particular."

After reading the rest of the report, Teph closed it the same way someone closes a book that just completely changed his outlook on life.

Teph's eyes were unfocused, staring off into the distance.

"Are you all right?" Richardson asked.

"Sorn is Nicoles. No, I'm not OK."

# FORTY-TWO

The warden's door swung open with such force that it slammed into the wall and cracked the window glass.

"You can't suspend me," Emil roared as he marched up to the warden's desk. "I *am* this prison. It doesn't exist without me!"

Warden Teph sat calmly behind his desk, despite the captain looming over him. Teph knew the captain was trying to draw him into a shouting match, but he refused to take the bait.

"You thought I was stupid," Teph said, narrowing his eyes. "You thought you could play me like a cheap violin. Well, the game is over."

"What game?" Sorn said, feigning ignorance. "What are you talking about?"

Teph was quietly amazed at this man's ability to deny everything.

"I know everything ... Nicoles."

Sorn blanched for a moment, then he smiled.

"Prove it. You don't have anything. This is just a bluff, hoping I'll admit to something you know nothing about."

"I have a large folder with your name on it," Teph said, tapping a folder on his desk.

Sorn looked at the folder and then at Teph. In a flash, he lunged for it but Teph was quicker. He grabbed the folder and threw it to the floor with his left hand. In the same motion he used his right to slam Sorn's head into the desk and dig his fingers into the nerve cluster behind the ear.

Sorn screamed in pain and flailed helplessly as Teph grabbed Sorn's left wrist and yanked in up into the middle of his back. His face shoved into the desk, all he could do was blindly flail at air, hoping to get a hold on Teph.

"Now," Teph grunted. "You are suspended pending criminal charges."

Then he let him up. Emil sprang up and reached for his baton. Teph stood in a defensive stance but said nothing. He silently dared Emil to make a move. Three sheriff's deputies burst in from the side room where they had been waiting. They grabbed Emil and cuffed him before he could react. He struggled, but they tased him and dragged him out.

"Repairing that window will come out of your final paycheck," Teph yelled at Emil as he was taken out. Emil pretended he didn't hear him.

~

Everyone expected the trial to be a slam dunk. Emil had been arrested without much incident and held in the Larsan County Jail in lieu of $1 million bail. The story spread like wildfire, locally and nationally.

*Captain Carnage* is what the media dubbed him. Vegas even had a line on the trial. People were betting on a speedy trial and guilty verdict ending in a death sentence.

The media circus was amazing. Larson County was inundated with reporters who swarmed in from all over the country. Between the media and the inmates' family members, the population of Larsan swelled by nearly two thousand people overnight. The jail only had forty cells, and Emil's was quickly identified. Reporters crowded around his window asking him questions night and day.

Hundreds of people crowded the lawn, street, and parking lot around the jail. Pictures, posters, and signboards were paraded around, each with the face of an inmate on it. At night, candles burned and people sang. People who didn't know about this case would've thought that these pictures were of righteous martyrs killed in battle or sacrificing themselves for some great cause. They would have no idea that each picture was of some criminal who had committed murder, rape, assault, or even more grotesque crimes. Emil had to grit his teeth every time he looked out the window, which wasn't often.

Judge Sawyer Bradley sat quietly in his study at 9:30 p.m., researching an obscure murder case, seeing if there was a legal precedent that might have bearing in the Emil Sorn trial. Sawyer was in his early sixties. He had been a judge in Larsan County for 32 years. He would've retired last year if his wife of 47 years hadn't up and died on him. Having nothing to look forward to, he just kept on working. He figured that one of these days he would just get tired of the nonsense and quit right in the middle of a trial.

*This Sorn trial is shaping up as a good candidate for that very scenario*, the judge pondered. A knock at the door interrupted his thoughts. He got up, tromped to the door, and ripped it open.

"I thought I told you people no interviews!"

A stocky man in his mid-forties stood there surprised at the reception.

"I'm sorry to disturb you so late, Your Honor," Sheriff Secrest said.

"Ted?" Judge Bradley said, embarrassed. "I'm sorry, I

thought you were one of those reporter vultures."

"No, sir. May I come in? I need to talk to you."

"Of course."

He ushered the sheriff into the sitting room.

"Can I offer you a drink? Scotch? Bourbon?"

"No, sir, I'm still on duty."

"How about a beer then?"

"A beer would be great."

Bradley returned with a beer, and a scotch for himself.

"So, what brings you to the outskirts of Larsan?"

"Emil Sorn."

"I've heard that name way too much lately. Has he done something else? Has he escaped?"

"No, no, nothing like that, it's just these damn reporters. They swarm all over the jail like bees on a honeycomb. They try to talk to him through the window. They try to sneak in to see him. I nearly had to tase a reporter today because she refused to leave the jail without speaking to him. She said it was her constitutional right."

"So, what happened?"

"Let's just say you have a resisting arrest charge up next on your docket."

Bradley smiled.

"Bravo."

"It's just that every day they get a little closer, a little sneakier, a little bolder."

"It is a problem," Bradley said, sipping his scotch.

"That's not even mentioning the death threats from the victims' families," Ted said. "They hang out just behind the reporters, constantly being interviewed and making themselves more and more angry. They started throwing rocks at the jail last night. I wonder when they'll start throwing grenades."

"So, what are you saying, Ted?"

"You know I'm no shirker."

"I know."

"I pull my weight around here."

"Absolutely."

Ted seemed to deflate a little.

"I just don't think we can protect him much longer."

"What would you have me do?"

"Move him out of county, do a change of venue, anything to get him out of my jail."

Bradley quietly pondered this for a few moments.

"What about the state prison?"

"You mean put him back with his own people?" Ted said. "Isn't that dangerous? What if they help him escape?"

"Quite frankly, I hope they try."

"What?"

"I hope he tries to escape and is shot dead. That way I won't even have to hear this travesty."

"You're not serious?"

"I'm dead serious," Bradley said. "This monster has made a mockery of the justice system and did it believing he was one hundred percent in the right. I want him dead before more like him pop up, and soon we have a country full of vigilantes administering their own 'justice' without the law."

The two men sat silent nursing their drinks.

"Do you think what he did was right?" Ted asked.

The judge thought about it for a few minutes.

"The law says he was wrong," the judge said slowly.

"That's not what I asked."

"Is this off the record?"

Ted looked hurt.

"Sir, when have any of our talks like this been on the record?"

"You're right, of course," Bradley said, looking abashed. "My apologies."

"So, you believe he was right?"

"I believe it's going to be a very interesting trial."

Sensing that the conversation was over, Ted finished his beer and started toward the door.

"Thank you for the drink and the conversation."

"Anytime," Bradley said, walking him to the door.

"So, you'll take care of the paperwork?"

"I'll start it tonight. You can take him to the prison tomorrow."

"Thank you, Your Honor."

"You're welcome, Ted. Good night."

# FORTY-THREE

W here are you taking me?" Emil said from the back seat of the squad car as they drove out of town.

"You'll see," Sheriff Secrest said.

Five minutes later they pulled into the parking lot of Larsan State Prison.

"Oh, hell no!" Emil growled, struggling against his handcuffs and kicking the front seat.

"Look," the sheriff said, "would you rather stay here and be isolated from everyone, or would you rather have reporters beating on your windows day and night?"

Emil paused. He hadn't slept much in the last few nights, mostly because of the media.

"Let me ask you, Sherriff," Emil said. "If our roles were reversed, would you want your men to see you like this?"

Sherriff Secrest appeared conflicted.

"Wait here," he said, leaving the deputy to guard Emil in the squad car. Thirty minutes later he came back to the car, and they drove through the gate for processing. Warden Teph met them at the door and ushered them into a side room.

"Mr. Sorn," the warden said, "good to see you again."

Emil just glared at him, refusing to speak. The tension in the room was like a living thing, a storm cloud of rage waiting to burst.

The sheriff cleared his throat.

"Mr. Sorn," he said, "the warden has graciously agreed to some provisions, due to the special circumstances of this case."

"Such as?" Emil said, without taking his eyes off Teph.

"Housing you in the protective custody wing, where you would have more privileges and access to the law library."

"And what would be the cost of this accommodation?" Emil said, continuing to glare at the warden.

"Names," Teph said.

"I have several names for you, all with four letters," Emil said.

The corner of Teph's mouth quivered into the slightest of grins in spite of himself.

"Cute. I was thinking more along the lines of officers involved with your little shadow gang."

This time Emil's smile was as wide as the Cheshire cat's.

"It haunts you, doesn't it?" Emil said. "Knowing that my *shadow* gang is still here, invisible, waiting. How are you sleeping at night knowing that one-on-ones could start back up again at any time?"

The mask of calm that Teph wore gave in to one small crack. He twitched for just an instant, but Emil saw it and pushed even harder.

"So, let's recap," Emil said, looking smug. "You want me to rat out my fellow officers in exchange for being housed with a bunch of child molesters?"

"Essentially correct."

"I'd rather go to the hole."

"That can be arranged."

"You better bring a lot of officers," Emil threatened.

## CHAPTER 43

"I thought that's what you would say," Teph said, nodding toward the sheriff.

Emil felt a sting in his neck. His eyes became unfocused, and the room swam as he lost consciousness. When he awoke two hours later in an RHU cell, Warden Teph was waiting at the door.

"Good morning," he said. "I apologize for the tranquilizer, but I was protecting my officers. I know you understand that."

Rage burned hot in Sorn's eyes as he looked around his cell searching for something to throw at the door. He spotted a small wooden desk and chair.

"I wouldn't do that," Teph said, as if reading his thoughts. "That desk and chair have been put in your cell as a courtesy. In the drawer are a pencil, a legal pad, and all your legal paperwork. If you destroy it, I will not replace it."

"You have to!" Sorn seethed.

"I don't and I won't. Behave, prepare your case, and you will be treated well. If you don't, you will be marched through this prison three times a day, naked."

"You're bluffing."

Teph leaned close to the door.

"You played me for a fool, disgraced your uniform, and murdered people for your own twisted pleasure," Teph said. "You have no idea what I would do to you."

They held each other's gaze for a moment. Then Teph turned and strolled back to his office.

Emil slowly walked over to the desk, sat down and pulled the pad out of his drawer. He stared at the yellow paper for a few minutes. After calming down, and gathering his thoughts, he began to write.

*To: Mr. Able Williams, Senator.*

*Dear Senator Williams, I'm not sure if you remember me, so I'll give you a brief reminder ...*

# FORTY-FOUR

The courtroom was packed beyond capacity. It seemed that every family member of every inmate who had been hurt or killed at Larsan was in the courtroom. The sheriff had to call in every reserve deputy he had, just to enforce courtroom security. Emil arrived at the back of the building and was treated to the sight of dozens of reporters running around from the front screaming questions at him, tripping over each other's microphone cords, and yelling at their own camera operators to hurry up. It looked like a media version of keystone cops. Emil did everything he could to delay things so he could talk to the reporters, but the deputies were trying to drag him in before the media got there.

"Police brutality!" he screamed toward the approaching reporters. "I was drugged and held against my will at Larsan State Prison. My constitutional right to a fair trial is being denied."

They dragged him through the back door and slammed it shut, pausing just inside the door. Five deputies and the sheriff were all breathing hard.

"Sorn," Sheriff Secrest said, angry and out of breath, "did you ever read *A Time to Kill?*"

## CHAPTER 44

Emil thought for a moment.

"No, but I saw the movie. Hated the ending; he should've fried."

"Well, if someone jumps out and points a gun at you, we will use you as a human shield," the sheriff said. "So, quit this nonsense, or I swear I'll shoot you myself."

Emil eyed him for a moment and then slowly walked forward, allowing himself to be ushered down the hallway toward the courtroom. He noticed how many doorways and blind corners there were in this courthouse.

When Emil entered the courtroom, it resembled a professional wrestling match more than a trial. Cameras immediately began flashing in Emil's direction, and a loud chorus of "boos" seasoned with more than a few screamed expletives reverberated off the walls. As more people realized that Emil was in the room, the din grew even louder. Deputies trying to quiet people had their hands full and were quickly shouted down. No one heard the bailiff yell, "All rise!" when the judge entered the courtroom.

For his part, Judge Bradley was shocked when he stepped from his chambers. He actually looked at the brass plate on the door to make sure he was in the right place. Sure enough, it said, "Courtroom One." He stepped through the doorway and paused to survey the sea of bodies. It looked like a combination of a rock concert and soccer riot.

The bailiff and two deputies stood between Emil and the crowd, forming a human wall. The noise was so deafening that no one could hear Judge Bradley banging his gavel and yelling for order.

After five useless minutes of trying to calm the crowd, the judge caught Sheriff Secrest's eye and motioned him up to the bench. After some brief instructions, which had to be shouted, the sheriff disappeared. He returned five minutes later and handed the judge a bullhorn. The judge turned on the siren and let it blare until everyone was covering their ears. Finally, the room became quiet.

"I understand that this is an emotionally charged case," the judge said quietly, so that people had to strain to hear him. "But I simply will not stand for these outbursts. From this moment on, anyone other than me, the attorneys, or the witnesses, who speaks above a whisper will be removed from this courtroom. Is that understood?"

Murmurs of dissent echoed through the room.

"Quiet," the judge screamed, banging his gavel. "Now, if everyone will calm down and sit down, we can get this trial started. Is everyone ready?"

Nods all around from prosecution, defense, and jury.

"Docket number one three one seven one seven: The People versus Emil Juan Sorn. Mr. Sorn, please stand."

The judge's gavel quickly silenced muffled boos.

"Mr. Sorn, you have been accused of the following charges. Four counts of first-degree murder. Fifteen counts of second-degree murder. Thirty-three counts of conspiracy to commit murder. Seven counts of attempted murder. Fifty-one counts of aggravated assault. Nine counts of manslaughter. Fifty-seven counts of assault with a deadly weapon. Thirty-seven counts of assault and battery. How do you plead?"

"Not guilty," Emil announced.

The courtroom exploded with screams of defiance. People shouted threats of lawsuits, bodily harm, even death. The media ate it up like vultures crowded around a pile of rotting flesh. Cameras shot anything and everything they could—wide shots of the unruly crowd, close-ups of Emil standing confidently, deputies trying to hold back the crowd.

"Clear this room," the judge ordered.

# FORTY-FIVE

When the dust settled, all that remained in the courtroom were the judge, jury, court personnel, the attorneys for the prosecution and defense, and Emil. The courtroom had an eerie feel to it, like the hangman was already waiting outside.

Larry Kinsinger rose. An up-and-coming young attorney in the DA's office, had begged, bribed, and pulled every string he could to get this case. Everyone told him not to take such a high-profile case for his first jury trial. They warned him to get a little seasoning first, get used to the courtroom and how to talk to a jury. Larry ignored them, of course. He had stars in his eyes. This case was widely known to be an easy win, and Larry wanted to start his career looking like a hero.

Kinsinger flashed his best smile and winked at the defense attorney.

Otis Lafferty was in his mid-fifties, short, balding, but well built, and charismatic when he chose to be. He hadn't chosen to be for a long time. He had been the public defender in Larsan for over twenty years. He had long ago lost his passion for his occupation. This Emil Sorn case, however, presented him with a unique situation. He believed Emil was guilty as sin; but, he had to defend him. In Otis's mind, he had two choices ... defend him so poorly that he would be removed from the case, or defend the case so well that Emil got off scot-free, proving what a great litigator he was and setting himself up to run for judge when Bradley finally retired. The problem with option two was that the people of Larsan didn't want to see Emil set free; they wanted to see him fry.

"So," the judge said, "if we can continue without interruptions, I believe Mr. Sorn entered a plea of *not guilty*. Defense, call your first witness."

"The defense calls Emil Sorn," Lafferty said.

Emil strode to the witness chair. There the bailiff presented a Bible and Emil placed his right hand on it.

"Do you solemnly swear to tell the truth, the whole truth, and nothing but the truth so help you God?"

"I do," Emil said.

"Be seated."

Lafferty approached Emil with a wry grin on his face.

"Mr. Sorn, how long have you worked at Larsan Prison?"

"Seventeen years."

"And in that time, have you ever had to deal with an incident where an inmate assaulted another inmate?"

"Many times."

"And why do they assault each other?"

"Could be any reason. Gang rivalry, failure to repay a debt, lover's quarrel."

This brought a rumble of chuckles from the jury.

"Order," the judge said.

The jury quieted and Lafferty continued.

"And did any of these incidents result in injury to one or more inmates?"

"Most of the time, yes."

"Where would these inmates assault each other?"

"Wherever they had the opportunity?"

"So, there are places in the prison that aren't monitored by officers or cameras?"

"Unfortunately, yes."

"And do the inmates know where these blind spots are?"

"Better than the officers do."

"So, you're saying that it's not impossible for an inmate to beat another inmate to death without anyone in authority knowing about it?"

"Yes."

Lafferty shot a look over at the Prosecuting attorney who was scribbling notes furiously.

"What else could an inmate do without being caught?"

"I suppose if they worked in the kitchen they could poison a certain inmate's food."

"Objection," the prosecution said. "Defense is clearly leading the witness."

"Make a point, Mr. Lafferty," the judge said.

"My point is that inmates do some rather nasty things when they're so inclined. It's entirely possible that my client has been accused of some of those things that were committed by an inmate. Perhaps out of revenge, perhaps looking for monetary gain, perhaps just because they didn't like him. I would like the jury to consider this in their deliberations."

The silence hung heavy in the air. The jury regarded Emil, they seemed to ponder the defense's argument.

"I'm done with the witness for now, your honor," Lafferty said.

"Prosecution, you'd like to cross examine?" Bradley said.

"Yes, your honor," Kinsinger said.

"So, Mr. Sorn, how many people have you killed?"

The defense attorney leaped out of his chair like he was sitting on a spring.

"Objection!"

"Sustained," Judge Bradley said.

"All right, Mr. Sorn, how many people have you injured?" Kinsinger said without missing a beat.

"Objection!"

"Sustained," the judge said. "Mr. Kinsinger, approach the bench."

The judge leaned forward so that only the attorney could hear.

"I know you think you are some big shot rookie lawyer from the big city and we are just a bunch of country bumpkins, but I assure you, we know the law. So, build your case the way you're supposed to, or I will remove you from it. Is that understood?"

"Yes, sir."

Kinsinger walked slowly back to the witness stand, gathered his thoughts and started over.

"Mr. Sorn, are you familiar with the name Frank Carson?"

Sorn flinched.

"I've heard of it, yes."

"You've heard of it? Isn't that the name of the man who murdered your father in cold blood?"

"Yes."

"Have you ever visited the Larsan Cemetery?"

"Once or twice."

"Really?" Kinsinger said. "Isn't that where your father is buried?"

"Yes."

"The father that you loved so dearly and mourned for so long?"

"Your point?" Sorn said.

"Don't you visit two graves every year on the same day?"

Sorn sat motionless, refusing to answer.

"Don't you visit your father, then visit Frank Carson?"

Sorn pretended not to hear him.

"Don't you go to Frank Carson's tombstone every year, just to urinate on it?"

No response.

Kinsinger leaned close.

"I bet it bothers you that Frank died before you could get him in your little torture chamber."

"Objection!"

"Sustained."

"Let's move on to another name," Kinsinger said, nonplussed. "Dustin Brennley. Ring any bells?"

"One or two," Sorn said, his face beginning to flush.

"One or two? The man who raped your wife? I'm sorry, ex-wife. Didn't that make you even a little bit angry?"

"Maybe," Sorn said, trying to remain composed.

"How about Anthony Morrilli?"

"Morrilli was self-defense," Sorn screamed, jumping to his feet.

"Order!" Bradley yelled, banging his gavel. "Sit down, Mr. Sorn."

"Yes, sir."

"Mr. Kinsinger, bring this line of questioning to a point, quickly."

"Just one more name, Mr. Sorn," Kinsinger said. "Raymond Perry."

Sorn sat quietly, trying to look impassive.

"No answer?" Kinsinger said. "I didn't think so. All of these are names of people who are dead. In each of these cases, Mr. Sorn was involved. None of these cases went to trial until today."

Sorn shifted uncomfortably in his seat.

"How is that even possible?" Kinsinger asked Sorn. "Four wrongful deaths, not one trial? It appears you have a great deal of influence, Mr. Sorn."

"Objection!"

"Sustained," Judge Bradley said, glaring at Kinsinger.

Withering under his gaze, Kinsinger said, "No further questions."

Lafferty rose slowly and deliberately and approached the witness stand.

"Mr. Sorn, have you ever been assaulted during your time at Larsan Prison?"

"Yes."

"How many times?"

"Oh, too many to count."

"And have you ever had to be sent to the hospital for injuries due to these assaults?"

"Yes, once."

"For an extended stay?"

"Over a month."

"Wow, you must have been severely injured."

"They said it was touch and go for a while."

"And what happens to the inmates who commit these assaults?"

"They are given a hearing and if found guilty they go to RHU."

"RHU, I'm not familiar with that term. Would you explain it to me?"

"RHU is the restricted housing unit. It's slightly smaller than a normal cell, about six feet by ten feet, with no window. When an inmate is there, they receive fewer privileges than in their normal cell, and their movement is restricted."

"Does that mean you tie them up in their cell?" Lafferty asked, half afraid of the answer.

"No, it means they can't attend church, library, or other programs while they're in RHU."

"Really? That's it?"

"They could get more charges if it was bad enough."

"So, the punishment for assaulting an officer is a slightly

smaller cell and you don't get to go to church?"

"Essentially, yes."

"Do they receive any physical punishment?"

"No."

"Thank you, Mr. Sorn. No further questions."

# FORTY-SIX

"Prosecution calls Alice Macgregor-Sorn."

Alice sauntered up to the witness chair. Even in her business suit, her curves still drew attention. Several of the male jurors felt the temperature in the room suddenly rise a few degrees.

"Do you swear to tell the truth, the whole truth, and nothing but the truth?" the bailiff asked.

"Yes."

"Be seated."

"Mrs. Sorn—" the prosecutor began.

"It's Ms. Macgregor," she interrupted.

"Excuse me," Kinsinger said. "Ms. Macgregor. How did you first meet the defendant?"

"At work."

"And how long were you married to Mr. Sorn?"

"Six months."

"Six months?" he repeated. "That doesn't seem very long."

"No, sir, it doesn't," she said, looking at Emil sadly.

"So, in the time you were married to Mr. Sorn, did you ever see him do anything improper?"

"You mean at work?"

"Yes, ma'am."

She thought for a long moment.

"Define improper."

Kinsinger rolled his eyes.

"Anything that was against the rules, anything of questionable morality, anything that just didn't seem right."

Alice started to laugh.

"Have you ever been inside a prison?" she asked Kinsinger.

"No, ma'am. Just answer the question, please."

"Corrections is like no other profession. We have to deal with the lowest of the low, the people society doesn't want to deal with or know about, and we have to do it professionally. Even when we are being treated very unprofessionally. When we get spit on, beaten, raped, killed, we still have to be professional."

"That is correct," Kinsinger said. "So, did you ever see Mr. Sorn act unprofessionally?"

She looked at Emil, who seemed to have just the slightest of grins tugging at the corner of his mouth.

"Your Honor, do I have to answer that?" she asked. "Can't I invoke my Fifth Amendment rights?"

"Would your answer incriminate you?" Judge Bradley asked.

She thought about it for a long moment.

"No, I don't think so."

"Then, you have to answer the question."

"And what happens if I don't?"

"Then I could hold you in contempt of court and send you to jail for an unspecified length of time."

"I understand," she said.

She stared at Emil for a long time. It seemed as though they were having a mental conversation no one else was privy to. Finally, Kinsinger cleared his throat.

"Well, Ms. Macgregor?" he said. "Did you ever see Mr. Sorn act unprofessionally?"

"No," she answered quickly and emphatically.

It was the last thing Kinsinger expected to hear.

"You realize that you're under oath?"

"Yes, I do," she said confidently. "And I have answered your question. May I go now?"

Kinsinger was just frustrated enough that he was about to let her go, when a thought occurred to him.

"Did you ever hear of Mr. Sorn acting unprofessionally?" he asked.

She shifted in her seat, but did not answer.

"Objection, Your Honor," Lafferty said.

"Hold on," Judge Bradley said. "I want to hear this."

Kinsinger smiled.

"Ms. Macgregor?" he said, with sickly sweetness.

She hung her head.

"Yes," she said, barely audibly.

"I'm sorry, I couldn't hear you."

"I said, yes. I have heard of Emil doing unprofessional things."

"Such as ..."

"Such as putting a hit out on an inmate."

"Really?" Kinsinger said. "Planning the murder of an inmate? And who told you about this hit?"

"He did."

"I'm sorry, you mean Mr. Sorn told you himself that he was going to kill an inmate?"

"No, that he had already done it."

Kinsinger was far more surprised than he let on.

"And who was this inmate?"

"Dustin Brennley."

Kinsinger turned toward Sorn and said, "Ding, ding."

Sorn nearly flew over the table at him and had to be restrained.

"All right, counselor. You've made your point. Move on," Bradley said.

"Thank you, Ms. Macgregor, you're excused. Prosecution calls Mr. Alfred Tanzey."

Tanzey walked to the witness stand and was sworn in.

"Mr. Tanzey, how long were you the warden of Larsan Prison?" Kinsinger began.

"Five years."

"And during your tenure as warden, did Mr. Sorn serve in any supervisory role?"

"Yes, he was a sergeant when I arrived and became captain just before I left."

"Wait a minute," Kinsinger said, looking confused. "Sergeant ... to captain? That's quite a promotion. What happened to lieutenant?"

"Mr. Sorn had been passed over for promotion several times through a series of oversights."

"And you felt it was time to even things out," Kinsinger said. "Settle the score, as it were?"

"Yes, that's correct."

"Was that the only score you were settling?"

"Excuse me?" Tanzey said.

"What is your relationship with Alice Macgregor-Sorn?" Kinsinger said, ignoring Tanzey's comment.

"I have no relationship with Ms. Sorn."

"Did you have one in the past?"

Tanzey hesitated, looked over at Emil, and then finally answered.

"Yes."

"And was this relationship while Ms. Sorn was married?"

"No."

"Before or after?"

"After."

"And how long did this relationship go on?"

"About three months."

"Did it become physical?"

"Meaning?"

"Meaning, did you have sex with Ms. Sorn?"

"Your Honor," Tanzey said. "Do I have to answer that?"

"Mr. Kinsinger," Judge Bradley said, "is there a point to this line of questioning?"

"Yes, sir."

"Get to it, quickly."

"Yes, Your Honor."

"Mr. Tanzey," Bradley said, "please answer the question."

Tanzey looked over at Emil and lowered his head slightly. He said, "Yes."

"So, you were in a physical relationship," Kinsinger said. "And you deeply cared for her?"

"Yes."

"Deeply enough to protect her?"

"Yes, of course."

"During your relationship, did anything traumatic happen to her?"

"She was raped."

"Oh my," Kinsinger said in mock horror. "That must have been terrible. Who was it who raped her?"

"Dustin Brennley."

"The same Dustin Brennley who was an inmate at Larsan Prison?"

"Yes."

"How did you handle that?"

"I investigated, had Mr. Brennley put in RHU, and filed criminal charges."

"And that's all you did?"

"What else was there to do?"

"Between you and me," Kinsinger said, "I would've beaten the hell out of the guy."

"I'm not allowed to do that," Tanzey answered stiffly.

"What happened to Mr. Brennley?" Kinsinger asked. "Did he go to trial for this?"

"No, he fell ill and passed away."

"And how long was this after Mr. Brennley raped Ms. Sorn?"

"About two weeks."

"Did Mr. Sorn have access to Mr. Brennley?"

"Yes."

"How long after Mr. Brennley's death was Mr. Sorn promoted to captain?"

"Around ten days."

"And how long after that did you retire?"

"About three weeks."

Kinsinger took a deep breath, then slowly walked over to the jury box and addressed the jury.

"So, let's recap," he said. "You were in a physical relationship with, and cared deeply for, Mr. Sorn's ex-wife," Kinsinger said, beginning to tick off points with his fingers. "An inmate rapes the woman you love, is sent to RHU, then suddenly dies under suspicious circumstances. After which, Mr. Sorn is suddenly promoted to captain, and you retire."

"Is there a question in there that I'm supposed to answer?" Tanzey asked.

"Yes," Kinsinger said, walking slowly up to the witness chair and stopping inches away from Tanzey.

"Did you use your position as warden to make a deal with Mr. Sorn for Mr. Brennley's death, in exchange for a promotion?" Kinsinger said slowly.

"Your Honor," Tanzey said. "I would like to invoke my Fifth Amendment right and not answer that on grounds that it may incriminate me."

"You have that right," Bradley said. "You don't have to answer."

Instead of being disappointed, Kinsinger actually wore a smile. He walked back to the jury box and said, "Thank you, Mr. Tanzey. You've told us all we need to know."

Walking toward his seat, strutting like a conquering hero, Kinsinger leaned over to Lafferty and said, "Your witness."

Lafferty slowly got up and made his way to the witness stand.

"Mr. Tanzey," he started, "I know that the prosecutor has been very hard on you. I assure you I will not take such a toll. In fact, I only have three very simple questions."

Tanzey visibly relaxed.

"OK."

"Mr. Tanzey, did you ever see Emil Sorn do any physical harm to Dustin Brennley?"

"No."

"Did you ever give Emil Sorn a *direct* order to harm Dustin Brennley, in any way?"

"No."

"Last question," Lafferty said. "Before this trial, was Emil Sorn ever charged with Dustin Brennley's death?"

"No."

"I have no further questions. Thank you for your time." Lafferty turned and shot a brief grin at Kinsinger. For his part, Kinsinger did a remarkable job of looking impassive, but inside he was seething. He knew that he had built an amazing argument, the best argument he had ever built ... and yet, with three little questions it was falling apart like the Hindenburg going down in flames.

"Do you have any more questions for this witness?" Bradley asked Kinsinger.

"No, Your Honor."

"Then the witness is excused, and we will take a recess for lunch," Bradley said, banging his gavel.

The courtroom quickly cleared. In minutes, the only

ones remaining were Lafferty straightening papers, and Kinsinger brooding.

"Go ahead and gloat," he said without looking at Lafferty.

"For what?" Lafferty said, looking genuinely surprised.

"You won that round," Kinsinger said. "You took my best shot and turned it back on me."

"It wasn't easy though," Lafferty said. "You presented one hell of an argument."

"Thanks, but it wasn't enough."

"Come on, kid," Lafferty said. "I'll buy you lunch."

# FORTY-SEVEN

Later that day the trial continued.

"Prosecution calls Irwin Ryan Colton."

Colton shuffled into the courtroom wearing cuffs, shackles, and a cheap suit that the prison kept on hand for inmates to borrow for trial. He was seated and sworn in. Even in chains and a bad suit, he still had a regal air about him, as if nothing could keep him down. Kinsinger hated him immediately.

"Mr. Colton," Kinsinger said. "Did you share a cell in Larsan Prison with an inmate named Raymond Perry?"

"Yes, sir, I did."

"What happened to him?"

"He died," Colton said, his face impassive, showing none of the emotions that were simmering just beneath the surface.

"And how did he die?"

Colton hesitated.

"I was not a direct witness. Therefore, any opinion I state would be merely hearsay and inadmissible."

Kinsinger hated him a little more.

"I understand that," he said. "Please refrain from telling me how to do my job, and answer the question."

"Very well," Colton said. "I believe he was killed in a one-on-one."

"Objection."

"Sustained."

Colton raised an eyebrow, giving Kinsinger an, "I told you so," look.

Kinsinger swallowed his anger and continued. "So, what is a one-on-one?"

"It is a program designed by Mr. Sorn in which inmates are beaten into submission by their victims."

"Objection," Lafferty said. "How does this inmate know what was designed by Mr. Sorn?"

"Mr. Colton," Judge Bradley said, "how do you know if Mr. Sorn designed some elaborate torture system?"

"Because I helped him design it."

The courtroom went silent. If the judge had stripped naked, jumped up on his desk, and started dancing, there would have been less of a reaction. The only two who weren't shocked were Colton and Emil. Judge Bradley was the first to recover.

"I believe that we're going to need some more explanation," he said to Colton.

"A long time ago, I was a college professor," Colton started. "Mr. Sorn was a student in my criminal-justice class. I had begun to teach on alternative rehabilitation techniques in prisons. Mr. Sorn came up with a theory that the victims should be allowed to return harm to their attackers. I was intrigued by the concept and suggested that he write a paper on it. As he wrote it, he consulted with me several times."

Lafferty stood and cleared his throat.

"Um … Your Honor … the witness's rights …" he said, trying to be as humble as possible.

"Oh, yes," Bradley said. "Mr. Colton, I must inform you that by stating you assisted someone who is on trial, you may end up being charged as an accessory."

"I understand," Colton said.

"And do you wish to continue with your testimony?"

"Yes, sir."

"Very well then. Continue counselor."

"Let's talk about one-on-ones," Kinsinger said. "What is it that happens at a one-on-one?"

"Objection," Lafferty said. "How do we know this *one-on-one* even exists? This is all hearsay."

"I'll change my question, Your Honor," Kinsinger said. "Mr. Colton, what was involved in the concept that you and Mr. Sorn designed?"

"If I had an inmate acting up that was difficult to control, I would call the inmate's victim, or the victim's family. They would be offered the opportunity for some retribution, with a guarantee of no charges and no witnesses."

"What type of retribution?"

"Physical, with a little psychological thrown in for good measure."

"Such as ... ?"

"The victim using the same weapon they had been attacked with."

"Sounds interesting," Kinsinger said. "Has it been effective?"

"Let me put it this way," Colton said. "Since Mr. Sorn became captain, Larsan has gone from one of the loudest prisons with the most in-house crime to the quietest with the least."

"And how do you know that?"

"I talk to people—inmates, officers, visitors, whoever I can."

"So, everything you've just said; we're going on your word?"

"I suppose so."

"Just one more question," Kinsinger said. "What are you in prison for?"

"Murder."

"No further questions."

"Mr. Colton," Lafferty started. "Did you ever get taken to a one-on-one?"

"Yes."

"And what victim came to accost you?"

"Mr. Sorn."

"Did he assault you?"

"No."

"Did he threaten you?"

"Not directly, no."

"Then what did he do?"

"Interviewed me."

"Why?"

"My cellmate had just escaped, and he wanted to find out where he was going so he could get him back."

"Who was your cellmate?"

"Raymond Perry."

"So, you say inmates were assaulted at one-on-ones, and yet that didn't happen to you. Why not?"

"I can think of two reasons," Colton said. "One is mutual respect. Mr. Sorn recognized me the first time he saw me in Larsan and has never given me a hard time."

"What's the other reason?" Lafferty asked.

"I told him what he wanted to know, and I never give *him* a hard time. There was no reason to assault me."

"You mentioned mutual respect. Do you respect Mr. Sorn?"

"Absolutely."

Lafferty sensed that he was playing with dynamite and had made his point already.

"No further questions, Your Honor."

Just as the judge was about to excuse the witness,

Kinsinger jumped up. "Your Honor, I have one more question for this witness."

"Proceed," he said, impatiently.

"Mr. Colton, you said you respect Mr. Sorn. Why?"

Colton thought for a moment. "Most of it is pride. Pride in a student being able to see an idea from conception to completion. That's a lot rarer than you think."

"So, you believe in Mr. Sorn's theory of torturing inmates?"

"Objection!"

"We have established that it is Mr. Sorn's theory, and we've established that it is torture," Kinsinger said to the judge.

"Overruled."

This time Kinsinger flashed a smile at Lafferty. "Mr. Colton?" Kinsinger said.

"Yes, I believe in Mr. Sorn's theory. I believe that some people deserve to be punished more severely for the heinous crimes they commit."

"And what makes you think that?"

"Because I deserve it."

"So, you want to be tortured?" Kinsinger said, incredulous.

"I deserve it for my crime, but he won't do it. I don't know if it's out of mutual respect or his idea of a cruel joke."

"Or maybe for you it's worse not to be tortured," Kinsinger said, thoughtfully.

"Possibly."

"No further questions," Kinsinger said.

"Mr. Lafferty?" the judge said.

"No, I'm done."

"Then we'll adjourn for the day."

# FORTY-EIGHT

The following day court resumed bright and early. The sun had just risen, and it was going to be a glorious day outside. The jurors groaned as they were herded into the courtroom. Each one had somewhere else they'd rather be.

Judge Bradley also seemed to have lost a step or two as he entered the courtroom and took his seat.

"Does the defense plan on calling any witnesses on its behalf?" Judge Bradley asked.

"Your Honor," Lafferty said, "we believe it is the prosecution's job to prove guilt, and in my opinion, Mr. Kinsinger has done nothing of the kind. In fact, the defense has to wonder if the prosecution is going to continue to serve us a diet consisting of only circumstantial and outdated evidence, expecting us to swallow it."

Kinsinger winced, knowing Lafferty was right. He silently weighed his options.

"Your Honor," Kinsinger said. "I have one further witness to call; however, I request a recess to discuss the circumstances."

Bradley glared at Kinsinger, but he refused to flinch.

"Very well. Fifteen-minute recess."

Once in the judge's chambers, Lafferty came unglued.

"What the hell is this? You didn't have any more witnesses on your list!"

"That's why it's called a surprise witness. I would think an old-timer like you would know that."

Lafferty was livid. He knew he had this trial all sewn up. And this snot-nosed little punk attorney was cheating.

"Enough!" Bradley said. "I'm tired of this trial. I want it over!"

"I swear, Your Honor, this is my last witness," Kinsinger said.

Bradley eyed him.

"All right," Bradley said. "I'll allow it."

"Your Honor!" Lafferty squealed.

But the judge silenced him by raising his hand.

"Let me warn you, Mr. Kinsinger," Bradley said. "If this is some smoke-and-mirrors ploy, you can consider yourself in contempt of court right now."

"It's not, Your Honor. However, I am requesting a few special allowances."

"Such as …?"

~

The courtroom was cleared of all media and cameras, the jury was given special instructions, and the trial resumed.

"Would the prosecution call its final witness?" Judge Bradley said, strongly emphasizing the word final.

"Prosecution calls Harley Richardson."

Harley walked in wearing a dark suit and tie, hair trimmed and styled, looking like a professional detective. If looks could kill, he would've dropped dead as soon as Emil saw him.

Harley sat, adjusted his suit, and was sworn in.

"Mr. Richardson," Kinsinger began. "What is your profession?"

Richardson shuffled in his seat and cast a nervous glance at the jury.

"Don't worry, Mr. Richardson, they have already been informed," Kinsinger said. "It's just for the record."

Richardson visibly relaxed.

"I am a police officer," he said.

"And how long have you been a police officer?"

"Nineteen years."

"And have you ever worked undercover?"

"Countless times."

"During an undercover investigation, have you ever been assaulted?"

"Yes, sir, several times."

"And what did you do?"

"I filed charges against the perpetrator."

Lafferty began to have a quiet but animated discussion with Emil, as Kinsinger continued his questioning.

"Did you recently undertake an undercover assignment inside Larson Prison?" Kinsinger asked Richardson.

"Yes, I did."

"What happened?"

"I was threatened and assaulted."

"By another inmate?"

"No, by Emil Sorn."

"Objection!" Lafferty yelled as he shot out of his chair.

"On what grounds?" Judge Bradley asked.

Lafferty floundered. He started rifling through papers as though the answer would magically appear. Kinsinger watched in sheer enjoyment. He had to fight the urge to smile.

"Well?" Bradley said.

Lafferty's shoulders slumped.

"Objection withdrawn," he said quietly, sitting down.

"So, Mr. Richardson," Kinsinger continued. "Tell us about this assault."

"I was taken to a small gymnasium, cuffed to a metal chair, and beaten."

"Who would do such a thing?" Kinsinger said, feigning indignation.

"Emil Sorn and two other officers."

"Did they say anything?" Kinsinger asked. "Did they give you any indication as to why they were brutally beating you?"

"Because I was teasing Mr. Sorn."

"I'm sorry, did you say because you were teasing him?"

"I was calling him by his first name," Richardson said. "He doesn't like that."

"And what did he assault you with? His fists?"

"No, a night stick."

"So, let me get this straight," Kinsinger said. "Emil Sorn beat you with a hardened wooden club because you called him by his first name?"

"Yes, sir."

"What more needs to be said?" Kinsinger said to the jury. "Pure brutality. Your witness, counsellor."

Lafferty had been furiously scribbling notes on a pad and barely heard the prosecutor. He did not rise right away.

"Counsellor?" the judge said.

"Just one moment, Your Honor."

"Do you need a recess?" Bradley asked.

"No, Your Honor," he said, finishing his frantic notes. Then he rose and approached the witness.

"Mr. Richardson, you say you have been assaulted before in the line of duty."

"Yes, sir."

"In these previous instances, had you identified yourself as a police officer before you were assaulted?"

"Yes, I believe so, sir."

"Did you identify yourself to Mr. Sorn?"

"I'm not sure I understand the question."

"Did you tell Emil Sorn that you were an undercover police officer before the alleged assault?"

"Well, no, sir."

"Don't you think that would have been prudent?"

"No, sir. I was investigating reports of brutality."

"So, you went looking for brutality in a prison and when you didn't find any, you began antagonizing Captain Sorn, hoping to frame him."

"That's not the way it—"

"How many witnesses were there to this so-called assault?"

"Um ... three."

"Including Mr. Sorn?"

"Yes."

"If I put Mr. Sorn back on the stand, do you think he would agree with your assessment of this incident?"

Harley looked over at Emil with resignation.

"It's hard to tell what he thinks anymore," he said.

"Oh, that's right," Lafferty said, brightening. "I forgot that you went to school with Mr. Sorn."

"That's correct, sir."

"And how would you describe your relationship with Mr. Sorn during your school years?"

"I would say friendly."

"Friendly?" Lafferty said. "You mean the two of you got along?"

"Yes, I'd say we got along fairly well."

"So, you never teased him back then?" Lafferty said. "Never goaded him into a fight? Never beat him up?"

"Yes," Richardson said, hanging his head. "I was a bully in school, but—"

"But Mr. Sorn broke you of that, didn't he?"

"Yes, but—"

"The same way Mr. Sorn tried to break you of being a

belligerent inmate, by pulling you aside and talking to you."

"You mean talking with a wooden club?"

"Who witnessed it?"

"No one who's going to take my side," Richardson said.

"Have you ever been investigated by Internal Affairs?" Lafferty asked.

Richardson paused.

"Every officer has at one time or another."

"I'm not asking about every officer," Lafferty said. "I'm asking about you."

After a long pause, Richardson sighed.

"Yes."

"Yes, what?"

"Yes, I have been investigated by Internal Affairs."

"For what?"

"That's none of your business!" Richardson snapped.

"Objection, Your Honor," Kinsinger said. "Is this pertinent?"

Judge Bradley pondered for a long moment.

"The witness will answer the question," he said.

"Falsifying reports," Richardson said quietly.

"I'm sorry, I couldn't hear you," Lafferty said.

"I was investigated for falsifying reports," Richardson spat at Lafferty. "But I was acquit—"

"I have no more questions for this noncredible witness," Lafferty said, turning and walking back to his desk. "You are excused."

"If I may, Your Honor …" Kinsinger said, jumping out of his seat.

The judge nodded.

"Officer Richardson," he said, emphasizing the word officer. "Have you ever been charged with conduct unbecoming?"

"No, sir."

"Have you ever been charged with any crime?"

"No, sir."

"No further questions. You may be excused. Thank you for your time."

# FORTY-NINE

After a recess, the judge made sure that both parties were ready before beginning closing arguments.

"The defense may begin," Judge Bradley said.

Lafferty rose and approached the jury box.

"Ladies and gentlemen of the jury, in closing I would like to do a little demonstration for you. I have here two baseballs," he said, handing them to the foreman.

"On one is written the word 'justice.' As the jury members each examine this baseball, they will see that the only other marking on this ball is the official seal of approval from Major League Baseball. Now, I also have another baseball, which I will hand to the foreman to pass around. As you can see, this ball has only the word 'revenge' on it, with no other markings. Other than the markings, these balls are identical. They feel the same, they weigh the same, they look the same. In fact, the only real difference is the seal of approval on one ball and not the other."

Pausing, Lafferty gathered his thoughts.

"Let's say my wife is out walking late one night, and a man grabs her, drags her into an alley, and kills her. If I go out, hunt this man down, and kill him, it's called revenge, and I will go to prison for it. Now, if the police catch him, put him in jail, and after years of trials, decide he deserves the electric chair, it's called 'justice.' Do any of the jurors go to jail for it? Does the judge? No. Why not? Because they have the seal of approval stamped on their ball—the judicial system.

"Justice and revenge are the same thing. The only difference is that one is called, *legal*, and the other is not. My client took initiative to right some wrongs, and the only reason he is sitting in front of you today is because he didn't have the seal of approval."

Lafferty walked slowly back to his seat. Kinsinger got up carrying a large legal book. He walked to the jury box, while still reading.

"My colleague has given an impassioned argument," he said without raising his eyes. "Even if it's wrong, I cannot find any legal precedent where revenge is used to justify murder."

"However, right here," he said, holding up the book, "it says that murder is illegal. So, let's define murder. Murder is the willful act of taking another person's life. It doesn't matter how you twist it to try and justify it, murder is still murder. That is why Emil Sorn is sitting here today; not because he is some superhero, as the defense would have you believe, running around in tights, dispensing justice; but because he committed murder. Not once, but several times."

Kinsinger slammed the book shut and went back to his seat.

The jury room was the prison of the courtroom, someplace no one wanted to be. If the jury room was like hell, then the Emil Sorn jury room was like jet fuel and battery acid raining in hell.

Debates raged endlessly, mostly on the difference between what was right and what was legal. Alliances formed, almost launching a verdict, only to fall apart because of one stubborn juror. Heated discussions, bribes, and threats were the norm ... and that was just over where to order lunch.

For nine days they ranted, raved, and rebutted. Finally, on day ten they managed to reach a verdict. Somehow the media found out and immediately began crowding into the courtroom, followed closely behind by the families and hanger-on attorneys. When the judge entered the courtroom, he had a flashback of the first day of this trial. As soon as he entered the room, people began to quiet down. Inwardly Judge Bradley chuckled.

"Ladies and gentlemen, I appreciate your attendance. I understand this has been a long process, but in the end justice will be served."

The crowd gave a polite applause.

"I am counting on each and every one of you," he said, "to remain calm no matter what the verdict is. I have already shown that I am not afraid of clearing this courtroom. Please don't make me do it again."

Murmurs and assenting nods ran throughout the courtroom as the judge took his seat. Everyone began studying members of the jury trying to get some indication of what the verdict could be. Ten days of hell did wonders for their poker faces. The jurors were unreadable. They were just glad it was almost over.

"Has the jury reached a verdict?" Judge Bradley asked the foreman.

"We have, Your Honor," the foreman said. The courtroom held its collective breath as the foreman stood and handed the paper to the bailiff who handed it to the judge.

Judge Bradley looked at the paper, then cleaned his glasses, took a drink of water, and straightened his robe before handing the paper back to the foreman.

## CHAPTER 49

"Mr. Sorn, please rise," Bradley said.

Clearing his throat, the foreman read, "We, the jury, find Mr. Emil Sorn, not guilty ..."

That was as far as he got. Bedlam erupted like a hand grenade in a dynamite factory.

The judge screamed his voice hoarse and broke two gavels trying to get order. Every bailiff and deputy tried to keep the courtroom from becoming a full riot.

# FIFTY

The courtroom was in shambles. Desks were overturned, papers were strewn everywhere, and a chair had been thrown through a window. Judge Bradley stood behind his desk looking over the carnage.

*I should be on a fishing boat in Florida right now, catching more beers than fish.*

He collapsed into his chair and blew out a heavy sigh. His mind was already made up—this would be his last case. Instead of taking a nice long walk through the courtroom and reminiscing, all he could do was stare at the destruction.

*All this because of one man,* he thought as the maintenance crew filtered in to begin the cleanup. The judge slowly shook his head and slunk to his chambers.

Emil Sorn had not helped the matter. When the riot began, he stood and started blowing kisses to the crowd like he was some celebrity. Anyone who tried to attack him made a major mistake. Even handcuffed and shackled, he took on several attackers and screamed challenges for more. He had to be tased and dragged into a side room to remove him from the situation. Once he recovered, his attorney came in to talk to him.

## CHAPTER 50

Emil held up his hands. "You can uncuff me now."

"What for?" Lafferty said.

"Didn't you hear the jury? I'm innocent."

Lafferty suppressed a chuckle. "There's a lot of things you are, but none of them are innocent."

"They said, 'not guilty.'"

"We didn't hear all the charges. They have to declare you *guilty* or *not* on each charge."

"What?" Emil screamed, suddenly on feet. "They can't do that. They said, *not guilty*; I heard them."

"Emil, you need to focus," Lafferty said.

"Focus on what? Making sure the electric chair is plugged in?" Emil said, pacing back and forth in the bare interview room.

"You need to calm down and let me do my job. These outbursts of rage aren't helping your case."

Emil stopped and glared at him.

"Who do you think you are?" Emil said, focusing his eyes with a piercing stare.

"I think I'm the guy who's been cleaning up your messes," Lafferty said. "I think I'm the guy who just might have saved your butt from frying in the electric chair!"

Emil glared at him. "Wait a minute. I remember you. It's been bothering me the whole trial. I knew I knew you. You're the S.O.B. that got that murdering piece of trash Maklayne back on the streets on a technicality."

Emil moved uncomfortably close to the lawyer. "How did it feel when he started killing again? When he abducted that young boy and skinned him alive? How did you feel knowing you were responsible?"

Lafferty couldn't decide which was disturbing him more, Emil slowly advancing on him like a stalking lion or the turn the conversation had taken. He sat in silence, unreactive. Emil's advance stopped abruptly when he reached the end of his handcuff chain.

"How did you feel when he took that pregnant woman, cut out the ... "

"Enough!" Lafferty yelled.

Emil smiled, like a cat toying with a mouse. "Don't worry; I finished the job you started. Maklayne won't be bothering anyone anymore."

Lafferty glared at him in disgust. "You're a monster!"

Emil's Cheshire-cat smile broadened. "Why councilor, how judgmental of you. What ever happened to innocent until proven guilty? That's not very professional. Besides, I'm not the monster. I keep the monsters off the streets. I'm the man who does the job no one else wants to do, that no one else has the courage to do. I'm a freakin' hero! And you're fired."

Five hours later Emil sat once again in the defendant's seat. Aside from the judge, jury, and prosecution, the room was empty.

"Mr. Sorn, please rise," Judge Bradley said, slurring his speech a tiny bit. "Foreman, please read the verdict again."

"Yes, Your Honor," he said, standing up. "The jury finds the defendant not guilty of aggravated assault, not guilty of battery, guilty of murder."

Emil stumbled back and fell into his seat.

"We will hold a sentencing hearing tomorrow," Judge Bradley said, looking around his destroyed courtroom. "And I will take everything into account," he said, glaring at Emil. "Court is adjourned."

# FIFTY-ONE

Senator Able Williams began his career as a smart, ambitious attorney. Fresh out of law school, with an unbounded work ethic and unyielding political ideals, Able quickly climbed the professional ladder from lawyer to senior partner at the most respected law firm in his home town to state attorney general. When he got to that level, his ambitions magnified. He even considered himself a candidate for the oval office.

He brokered power to get what he needed and curried favor with people in important positions to further his ambition. His office walls were covered with pictures of him shaking hands with celebrities, senators, congressmen, even the odd president or two. He constantly crusaded against the unfair treatment of the elderly, gays, and inmates. He was respected for being a political idealist who stuck to his views and fought for what he thought was right.

Often, he would seem to preach, instead of speak, on the evils of right-wing extremism, gay-bashing, and the death penalty. Able was on the fast track to political advancement, and he was doing all he could to speed up the train.

Then came the day his nine-year-old daughter was kidnapped. The ransom was paid, and the incident was quickly hushed up. But those "in the know" knew that she had been tortured and raped.

When they caught the man, the trial was quick, quiet, and severe. He got three consecutive life sentences, because for Able to pull strings to get the death penalty would be to go against one of his strongest beliefs. The man's name was never released, and he was quickly taken to an unnamed prison to serve his sentence.

Able and his wife tried for years to help their little girl recover. They took her to the best therapists, doctors, and psychologists, but she was never the same. The one thing that made him feel a little better was the one thing he was most ashamed of.

Two years after the incident, he rode the sympathy vote right into a senate seat.

~

It was a beautiful spring day. Senator Able Williams drove his Cadillac STS to work. Driving down Pennsylvania Avenue, he opened his window to breathe in the smell of the cherry blossoms. He pulled into his building, passed through security, parked his car, and made his way to his office. His secretary was an intelligent, attractive woman in her late twenties, ambitious to advance her own career, yet patient enough to wait for opportunities. She greeted Able in a warm, yet businesslike manner that showed no sign of the affair they were having.

"Good morning, sir. I have your mail sorted and on your desk. Here are your phone messages, and you have a twelve o'clock lunch scheduled with Senator Graham."

"Thank you, Miss Newell. Outstanding performance, as usual," he said with a wink.

She blushed, ever so slightly.

"My pleasure, sir."

Able entered his office, crossed the room to his richly finished desk, and sat in his comfortable leather chair. He exhaled deeply. His career was exactly where he wanted it to be, but it had come at a terrible price.

He shook off the thoughts of his daughter's torment and began his daily routine. A letter, marked 'urgent,' sat atop the pile of correspondence in his in-box. The name on the return address caught his eye, and his breath caught in his throat. He hoped he would never encounter that name again. He considered tossing it into the trash, but thought better of it. He reached for the letter like it was a copperhead, slit it open and began to ready. Before he was half finished he crumpled the pages and sat seething, trying to regain his composure, the letter a hardball in his fist. At last his anger bled away, replaced by an emotion he hadn't embraced in a long, long time ... Fear.

He eyed the letter with suspicion and then shredded it page by page. Afterward, he closed his eyes and leaned back in his chair for a few minutes. He was so deep in thought over the letter that his intercom beeping startled him.

"Yes?" he answered, half annoyed.

"Sir, I'm sorry to disturb you, but I have a man on the phone who wants to talk to you," his secretary said. "He says he is a major campaign contributor."

"Well then, put him through."

"Yes, sir."

"Senator Williams, how can I help you?"

"Senator is it now? I remember when you were attorney general."

"Who is this?"

The stranger chuckled on the other end of the line.

"Surely you haven't forgotten me so quickly, after the

favor I did for you. I guess becoming a hotshot senator makes you forget about the little people who helped you out on the way."

Able did not like being toyed with.

"Good-bye, whoever you are."

"I wouldn't recommend that," the stranger said quickly.

"Why not? You're just playing a game, and I refuse to play."

"OK, you win. I'll just say two more words, and if they aren't important enough to continue, you can hang up."

Able's curiosity got the better of him.

"OK, two words."

"Henri Benouli."

The temperature in Able's office dropped. His mind went numb and his jaw froze in a rictus snarl. He wasn't sure if he was even still breathing.

Days, weeks, even years could've passed, and he wouldn't have known the difference.

"Are you still there?" came the tormenting voice.

It was too much for Able. Fear and rage welled up within him, melting the paralysis away. He tried to speak, but the struggle against the shock was so great, all he managed to get out was one raspy word.

"Sorn?"

"Ah, so you do remember me," he said with genuine happiness. "I was beginning to worry."

As the shock wore off, Able regained his composure.

"What do you want?"

"Well, Senator, I'm sure you've read the letters I sent you explaining my current circumstance."

"I never received any letters from you," Able lied, looking at the shredder.

"Really?" Emil said. "I sent you three, just to make sure you got them."

Able began frantically searching the stack of mail,

looking for the other two letters, but couldn't find them.

"So, what did these letters say?"

"They said that I was on trial and may need your help. Since the time I sent those letters I have been found guilty and I'm going to be sentenced tomorrow."

"I'm very sorry to hear that," Able said sarcastically. "What does that have to do with me?"

"I want you to get me out."

"What?" Able shouted. "I'm not going to get you out of a punishment you brought on yourself."

"Yes, you will," Emil said.

"I will not risk flushing my career down the toilet just because you played with fire for too long and finally got burned."

"Let's reminisce, you and I," Emil said calmly. "It was what, about two and a half years ago? I've witnessed hundreds, even thousands of inmates come and go through my prison, but not one like that. He arrived in the dead of night, surrounded as much by mystery as the armed guards that transported him. No name was given, no questions were permitted. He was escorted into the prison and disappeared. It wasn't until later that I found out he had been taken to an unused section of RHU and kept there by special orders.

"I made it my business to find out all I could about him. It took months, but I finally found out his name and his crime. That's about the same time that you contacted me through a mutual friend. I remember many things about inmate Benouli's one-on-one visit. I remember you bringing your eleven-year-old daughter in to face her attacker.

"I remember the look of utter terror in her eyes. I remember you putting a knife in her hands and asking her to exact the type of brutal revenge that most adults barely have the stomach for.

253

"I remember the look of disappointment in your eyes when your daughter dropped the knife and ran away sobbing.

"And I remember the hatred and rage that covered your face as you picked up the knife and began to slash his body to pieces. When you were finished, he was an inch from death, and you stood there covered in blood still holding the knife, but you couldn't deal the final blow. So, I did it for you. You argued that it wasn't necessary, but I told you that a man with such information is too dangerous to be left alive."

"So, you're blackmailing me? I could put you away for a long time for that."

Emil started laughing.

"I'm already hearing whispers of the death penalty. What do I care about you putting me away for a long time? That would just give me more time to write my memoirs. I think I'll call it *The Torturer's Apprentice: A Day in the Life of a Senator*. What do you think?"

"What exactly do you expect me to do?"

"Get me out of prison," Emil said. "I'm sure you've got people who owe you favors. Just pull a few strings."

"Like the ones you've trying to pull on me? I am not a parachute. You don't just pull on my string to have me pop out and rescue you."

"That's fine. I didn't think you'd do it. Sorry to waste your time."

"What game is this?"

"No game, I'm just gonna call your closest rival senator. I'm sure he could find some use for this information come election time."

Able sighed.

"So, you've got me neatly boxed in."

Emil smiled on the other end of the line.

"Do we have a deal?"

"I'll talk to the judge," Able said reluctantly. "But I can't promise any results."

"That's OK. At least I'll know you tried."

"Really?"

"No!" Emil screamed. "You get me released, or a minimum sentence, or I'll feed your career to the press. You got it?"

Able had all he could take. He slammed down the receiver so hard that it cracked the plastic.

His mind felt like a washing machine on high spin. His intercom beeped.

"What?" he shouted.

"Um ... sir, it's nearly twelve. You have a lunch appointment with senator Grimes."

"Cancel it! I have other things to attend to."

~

Back at Larsan Prison, Emil called for the officer and handed him back his cell phone.

"Thank you very much."

"No problem, sir. If it weren't for you, I wouldn't have this job." Then he looked quickly around and lowered his voice. "And between you and me, I think what you were doing was the right thing."

"Thank you, officer."

~

The sentencing hearing was scheduled for first thing in the morning. The courtroom was still nearly empty. No media or onlookers, except for one—Warden Teph. Judge Bradley had personally requested he be there.

The judge entered looking tired.

He slumped into his chair and stared at the back wall. The rest of the courtroom exchanged curious glances and waited patiently.

Finally, the bailiff cleared his throat.

"Are you all right, Your Honor?"

He started as though being awakened.

"Yes, I'm fine, thank you," he said slowly. "Let's get this over with."

He looked over at the defendant with a mixture of contempt and resignation.

"Mr. Sorn, please rise."

Emil silently obeyed.

"Normally a guilty charge of multiple murders would command several life sentences, possibly even the death sentence. Due to special circumstances, however, that is not the case today." Bradley sighed heavily. "I am sentencing you to five years in prison."

The jury gasped collectively, but a withering glare from the judge silenced them. Emil did his best not to show any emotion at all, for fear that the judge might change his mind.

"Court is adjourned," Bradley said, barely above a whisper.

While Emil was being escorted out of the courtroom, he caught Warden Teph's eye and said, "Thanks for the vacation. I'll see you real soon." As the room was being cleared, the judge got Teph's attention and motioned him into his chambers.

The judge collapsed into his chair behind his antique mahogany desk. He closed his eyes for a moment to gather his thoughts. When he opened them, Teph was still standing in the middle of the room looking uncomfortable.

"Have a seat, Mr. Teph." He then reached behind him, to a secret stash of alcohol. "Care for a drink?"

"No thank you, sir," Teph answered. The judge poured himself a drink, took a swallow, and leaned back in his chair. His eyes appraised Teph.

"The reason I called you back here is to thank you for

helping us out by housing Sorn during this whole mess."

"No problem, sir. I was glad to help."

"How long have you worked in corrections?"

"Eight years, sir."

"How do you feel about our justice system?"

"I don't like the results sometimes, but it's the only system we have."

The judge eyed him again, took another drink, then hesitated.

"I have been a judge for thirty-two years. I have seen some of the most incredible miscarriages of justice over the smallest detail ..." he trailed off, staring at his desk.

"I'm sorry, sir. I tried to do the best I could ..." Teph said, sensing a rebuke.

"This isn't about you. This is about justice. It may surprise you, but I believe in Mr. Sorn's theories. Criminals don't get the punishment they deserve, in most cases. A man could beat another man nearly to death, paralyze him for the rest of his life, and what happens? That man gets maybe five years in prison, where he is warm and taken care of. He gets three meals a day, a bed, cable TV, daily exercise, can buy almost anything he wants. It's a vacation for him. He doesn't have to worry about rent, bills, laundry, dishes, nothing. But his victim is paralyzed for life and will never be the same again. I agreed with Sorn's idea of punishment to fit the crime, but he took it too far, and if you and I don't do something about it, he will get away with multiple murders."

Teph eyed the judge warily.

"What are we talking about here, sir?"

"I should've retired years ago," he said to himself more than Teph. "Then I wouldn't be here for some snot-nosed senator to threaten my pension."

"I'm sorry, sir?"

The judge waved him off.

"It doesn't matter. What's done is done. Now it's up to you and me to make it right."

"Are you asking me to do what I think you are?"

"I'm asking you to do what your conscience tells you to."

Teph sat quietly for a moment contemplating what had just been said.

"I am officially retiring effective tomorrow. It's up to you to act or not. I'm done with this case, this town, and this state. By next week I will be living on a fishing boat."

Teph got up and started for the door.

"Enjoy your retirement," he said, then he walked out.

# FIFTY-TWO

After the hearing, Emil was scheduled to return to another prison in the morning. Warden Teph came to visit him before he left. He was in protective custody while at Larsan. An officer let the warden into Sorn's cell and locked the door behind him.

"Are you sure that's wise? Being locked in here with a dangerous inmate?"

Teph shrugged off the veiled threat.

"I handled you once, I can handle you again if I have to."

Teph looked around the cell. Everything was placed in an orderly fashion.

"I came here to talk to you before you went away."

Sorn growled. "Talk? About what? The new fashions on Bravo block?"

Teph ignored the baiting.

"I wanted to know why. Why did you feel it was your right or duty to take the law into your own hands?"

Sorn glared at him.

"Go away."

"Answer my question first."

"Why should I tell you anything?"

"Because you've wanted to for so long. You've never had an equal you could tell all this to. It's all been underlings following orders, no one to truly listen. To let it out."

"Let me ask you something," Emil said. "Did you ever do anything wrong; ever make a mistake?"

"Sure, my latest one was just last month, letting you lead me on with that stupid masquerade, looking for a man who didn't exist. If I hadn't made that mistake, Raymond Perry would still be alive."

"Raymond Perry was a piece of trash who deserved to die."

"That may be true, but you and I don't get to make that decision."

Sorn grinned. "I do."

"So, what makes you any better than Raymond Perry, or any of the hundreds of other inmates you've tortured or killed?"

"Because I'm not a stinking criminal."

"You're sitting in a cell, in an orange uniform."

"I am not a criminal! I did what needed to be done. What the so-called justice system wouldn't do."

"Play God?"

"No," Sorn yelled, slamming his fist into his bunk. "I've seen the human refuse infesting this place. Repeaters and predators that go right back to committing the same crimes as soon as they hit the streets. And when they get caught again and sent back here again, they treat it like a family reunion. I've read the things they've done. Then they brag about it to their convict buddies. And after bragging about the heinous things they've done to other people, they act like they're at the Ritz or Hilton, demanding this and that, and then threatening lawsuits on anyone who doesn't bow to them. And what about the lives they've destroyed? Who demands justice for their victims? Not in my prison! I taught them a lesson, and I'd do it again. To every last one of them. My only regret is that I didn't get to have the fun of torturing and killing them myself."

Sorn was breathing hard, his face a contorted mask of rage.

Teph deflated a little. "Be that as it may, it's not our job to overrule the justice system. Our job is care, custody, and control. That's as far as it goes."

Sorn looked at him with a gleam in his eye. "Torture and death are forms of control."

Teph understood now that the good, well-meaning officer who had started working at Larsan so long ago was truly gone. In his place was the monster standing before him. He also knew beyond a shadow of a doubt that Sorn would kill again and that his vengeance would know no boundaries. He had already crossed the line, and he had no interest in going back.

"So that's it? You feel fully justified to rob each of those inmates of the possibility of turning his life around and making something out of himself?"

"Never happen. Once an inmate, always an inmate."

"Yes, I suppose you're right," Teph said, looking pointedly at Sorn's orange uniform. A sadness crept over him as he thought about the hollow shell of a man sitting in front of him. He stared at this beast, feeling no anger or malice, but pity. He rose to leave.

"Did you get what you came for?"

"Yes."

"I'll see you in five short years," Sorn said with a smile.

The officer opened the cell and Teph walked out. "Goodbye, Captain," he said without looking back.

In the morning, the officers came to get Sorn.

"Time to go, sir," one of the officers said.

They cuffed him and started him down the hall. The inmates were eerily quiet when he walked by. No catcalls, no whistles, no threats, just utter silence. Sorn could feel every eye on him. The officers took him down a corridor to a room that he recognized very well.

He began to struggle.

"No, you can't! No! No!" he screamed as they shoved him through door 114. Even with him cuffed, the officers had the fight of their lives on their hands. Eventually, they got him close enough to cuff him to a small metal chair.

"I'm sorry, sir," one of the officers said, breathing hard as they left the room.

Sorn glanced around the darkened room that looked like an empty gymnasium. He had never seen it from this perspective before. It looked larger; the shadows stretching into eternity. Then one of the shadows moved, then another, and then another. Soon the whole room was alive with movement, but all just on the edge of his vision.

"Well, who is it? Let's get this over with!" he said.

The dance of shadows ended when the lights came on. As his eyes slowly adjusted to the brightness, he looked around the room. He started recognizing faces right away. Dozens, perhaps hundreds of inmates and former inmates filled the room. Each one of them had been to one-on-one visits. He saw inmates barely able to stand, some with casts still on, some missing an arm, leg, or eye. But each one was holding a weapon of some sort. Knives, chains, baseball bats, even sledgehammers. It was as if Dante himself had invited him to be the guest of honor in some hellish reunion.

Captain Emil Sorn felt no fear or remorse. The thought of begging never once entered his mind. Of all his memories, the one that flashed through his mind was his first day at Larsan when he shot inmate Morrilli in the chest, knowing that he was dead before he hit the ground. The thought made him grin. He realized on that day that he would die in uniform. It just never occurred to him that it would be in an inmate's uniform. The thought amused him.

He started laughing. He was still laughing as the inmates closed in around him, and the first blow fell.

An hour later, Warden Teph made an announcement over the intercom.

"One-on-one visits are over."

He slowly pushed the microphone aside, feeling no anger, no malice, only remorse.

The prison remained silent. No one spoke; no one shouted. If anything, a collective sigh of relief was all anyone heard. Colton sat quietly in his cell. His eyes fell to the Bible verse he had been reading. Romans 12:19: "Vengeance is mine; I will repay, saith the Lord."

He stared at the passage for a long time. Then he closed his Bible and leaned against the post of his bunk. As he closed his eyes, a single tear ran down his cheek.

# Epilogue

She pulled her car to the side of the road, stepped out into a foot of snow, picked up her mail, and continued to the garage. She trudged through the unshoveled snow into the small blue house that was in need of some repairs. She knew it, but was so tired from working a full-time and part-time job just to keep up with the bills. She threw the mail on the kitchen table and turned her thermostat from sixty-two to sixty-six, just to take the chill out of the air.

Her stomach growled. Too tired to cook, she pulled open the freezer and selected an entrée of microwavable spaghetti before collapsing into a kitchen chair to sort through the mail. As expected, there were several bills, which would have to wait until after payday, and a letter from a law office. She opened it, and a piece of paper fell to the floor. She absently picked it up and laid it on the table as she began to read the letter.

*Dear Mrs. Macgregor-Sorn,*

*We were sorry to hear about your husband's passing. We wish to convey our deepest condolences. As you know, your husband had a standard life-insurance policy, as did all officers working at Larsan Prison. Your husband had taken out extra coverage.*

*Enclosed is a check for the lump-sum benefit of his policy. We hope that this will be some small comfort during your time of loss.*

Alice looked at the check, and her jaw fell to the table. She rubbed her eyes and looked again.

$2,786,532.48.

## Six months later

He slowly walked down the street. He had a hard time focusing some days. Other days, he just lay on his cardboard box all day. It wasn't always like this. There was a time when he'd been considered a hero. They even gave him a shiny piece of metal with some brightly colored ribbon on it. That seemed like a lifetime ago. As with so many others, they patted him on the back as they were shoving him out the door. They had spent months—even years—training him to be a soulless killer.

Then suddenly, with no warning, they told him to become a civilian. But no one trained him how to be civil again. It was as sure as the sunrise that he was going to have trouble adjusting. He wasn't really shocked when he ended up in prison.

All he wanted was someone to help him readjust. He walked down the street, making a turn he hadn't made in months. He knew there was a row of abandoned buildings down here. What better way to end his life than as an unwanted man in an unwanted building. He turned the corner and noticed a sign he had never seen before.

*Larsan Center for the Mentally and Physically Abused.*

He walked up to the door.

"Is this someone's idea of a joke?" he said, mostly to himself. After a moment's thought, he shrugged his shoulders. "What have I got to lose?"

He opened the door and peeked inside. It looked like they were just moving in. Boxes were still stacked against the wall, and there weren't any decorations. A simple desk and a few chairs were the only furniture. Aside from that, the room was empty—no people, nothing else. He was about to chalk it up as a joke and walk to the next building to do his business, when a lady walked in the room. She seemed surprised to see him.

"I'm sorry," she said. "I didn't hear you come in."

"I'll leave," he mumbled.

"No, please," she said. "How can I help you?"

He considered turning away from her and leaving anyway, except that she was quite beautiful, and she was smiling at him. It had been a long time since anyone had smiled at him. Usually they just ignored him, or turned the other way.

"Please sit down," she said. "Tell me a little bit about yourself."

He noticed her name tag.

*Alice?* he thought. *The name doesn't really fit her.*

He shook the thought away and settled into a chair beside her.

"Well," he said, "It all started after I got out of the army."

~ ~ ~

# Special Thanks

I couldn't have written this book without a lot of help. I wanted to say thank you to all those who assisted me in one way or another.

My wonderful wife and family, for supporting me and always being there.

Dean Cook, Mike Battaglia, Ryan Mullins, Linda Engle, Tom Ens, Michael Cahill and all my wonderful friends on Fanstory.com. Daniel Keen, Brian Clark, David Kessling, Hilary Hauck and all my friends at The Inkwell, Mike Parker; who helped me immensely in the editing of this book, and all of my friends working at the Bedford County Jail.

And mostly, to God, who has somehow put up with my crap all these years and still continues to help me, even though I don't deserve it.

Also Available From:

# WordCrafts Press

**When Kings Clash**
*by J.E. Lowder*

**The Scavengers**
*by Mike Parker*

**Odd Man Outlaw**
*by K.M. Zahrt*

**Maggie's Refrain**
*by Marcia Ware*

**The Awakening of Leeowyn Blake**
*by Mary Parker*

**End of Summer**
*by Michael Potts*

**The 5 Manners of Death**
*by Dareden North*

**Home**
*by Eleni McKnight*

*www.wordcrafts.net*

CPSIA information can be obtained
at www.ICGtesting.com
Printed in the USA
BVHW041837190319
543108BV00009B/234/P

9 780998 941653